THE MARRIAGE DEAL

Kathleen Ryder

DEDICATION

For anyone who has ever found love in an unexpected place.

CHAPTER ONE

Millie left the building in a daze, her breath hitched, tears threatening to spill from her eyes. The main street of Maitland was bustling with people, as it always was on a Friday afternoon. Only three and a half hours drive from Sydney, it was a popular weekend getaway for a lot of city dwellers. When her grandfather had died, leaving her as the sole inheritor of the idyllic property that she had lived at since the age of thirteen, she had dreamed of turning it into a luxury wedding venue, a place where the bridal party could relax and refresh before the big day. A place where the ceremony and reception could be held, close enough to town for the wedding guests to travel without strain. Millie had even had a honeymoon cabin built onto the property, complete with a deck overlooking the lush property, perfect for relaxing in the outdoor spa or around the firepit. Unfortunately, as Millie was only just discovering, her grandfather had taken out a second, secret, mortgage on the property, which had now come due. Millie felt sick with the thought that she might be in danger of losing her home, her entire life was tied up in that property, every memory that she had ever made that was worth keeping, had been formed on that land. There was no way that she was going to lose it without a fight.

First, though, she needed answers. And a plan. Millie wove her way through the throng of tourists, her feet taking a well-worn path, headed for The Daily Grind, a quaint coffee shop always overflowing with people and laughter. She slipped through the door marked STAFF ONLY and donned a frilly white apron from the shelf behind the counter, waving hello to her friend as she went. She knew this coffee shop like the back of her hand, it had been in the Capel family for over thirty years. The owner's daughter, Rachel, had taken Millie under her wing the first day she had met her, Millie's first day of high school, midway through the term. When the other girls had mocked Millie for having the wrong uniform,

Rachel had defended her. They had been inseparable ever since. The rest of the Capel family had followed suit, and Millie had found herself surrounded by the love of a family, something that she had never known previously.

After high school the two friends had attended university together, choosing to travel each day rather than stay on campus, neither one wanting to have to leave Maitland. While Rachel had studied a Bachelor of Business, majoring in retail and management, Millie had studied a Bachelor of Communications, majoring in Event Management. Rachel had taken over the day to day running of the family business once she had graduated, something that Millie was always happy to help her with, without needing to be asked. Millie's plans of starting up her own event planning business had been put on hold once she graduated, instead of starting a new chapter in her life, she instead found herself having to say goodbye to a chapter of her life.

Her grandfather had suffered a stroke the weekend Millie graduated and required around the clock care, something she was honoured to provide, after everything that he had done for her. He never fully recovered, and eight months later he slipped away in his sleep. Millie would have been lost those first few months without her grandfather, had it not been for the Capel family. They felt her pain as if it were their own, adding her daily chores to their own load, never once commenting or complaining. It had been the hardest period of Millie's life, losing her grandfather. Even her brother, Joshua, having returned home on leave from the army, was unable to ease Millie's pain.

Millie had been thirteen and Joshua fifteen when they had come to live with their grandfather, following the death of their mother Caroline, in a car accident. It should have been tragic, but the truth was, Caroline had never been much of a mother, instead leaving Millie and Joshua to be raised by a bevy of nannies. Their father, Peter, Millie's grandfather's son, had died shortly before Millie's second birthday, and Caroline had wasted no time in marrying, and divorcing, a long line of men, each one richer than the last. Living with their grandfather had been the first stable home that Millie and Joshua had ever known.

A couple of weeks later, after laying their grandfather to rest, Millie and Joshua sat down and discussed the will and their plans for the future. Joshua supported Millie one hundred percent, having no doubt in her ability to both found and run, a successful wedding planning business. While their grandfather had left the house to Millie, he left the property to Joshua, and she was eager to have his support. In the end, they had decided that the best course of action would be for Millie to remain on the property and convert it into her idyllic wedding retreat venue, and for Joshua to return to the army to finish out his contract. Joshua's heart was never really in farming, he had always wanted to make a difference in the world, and he believed that he could do that by remaining in the army. They both knew that Tillie was never going to be a farmer either, which only left them with one other option, to lease the farm paddocks to someone else. Luckily for Joshua and Millie, the neighbouring farmer was looking for a way to increase his stock levels, and leasing their farm was the perfect solution for all involved.

Although Joshua returned to the army once everything was sorted out, he still returned every chance he got, being just as much tied up to Maitland as his sister was. He was due home at the end of the month, by which time Millie would have to either have an answer for the bank or be prepared to lose everything. Which is why she now found herself in The Daily Grind. If anyone would understand, would be able to help her to think of a solution, it would be Rachel. It wasn't until almost two hours later that Millie finally got a chance to speak to Rachel. The lunch crowd had just started to thin out, their stomachs full of delicious pasties and delectable cakes. Millie sank gratefully into a vacant booth, smiling as Rachel appeared with a tray laden down with steaming mugs of hot coffee, and plates of homemade lasagne and garden salad.

"Millie thank you; I really appreciate the help." Rachel smiled at her friend. "It has been frantic around here today, with Mum off sick, and the tourists all here for the long weekend."

"You know you never have to thank me," Millie brushed her friend's comments aside, "it is my pleasure to help you, you know that."

"I do. So," Rachel quirked an eyebrow in Millie's direction, "what's wrong? You look like you have seen a ghost. Oh no, is it your mum, is she back to cause havoc?"

"No, it's my grandfather. I had a meeting with the bank manager today my grandfather took out a second mortgage on the property, shortly after Josh and I arrived in Maitland. The loan documents weren't in his will or with his personal papers, I had no idea it even existed." Millie took a large slug of her coffee, needing fortifying.

"If I had only known about it Rachel, I could have been paying it off, instead of letting it sit there. There haven't been any payments into that loan in years, and it has now come due. The new bank manager only recently got to the loans, he has been busy settling in, whatever that means in a town this size. The loan is due, in full, by the end of the month, or else I lose everything."

"No!" Rachel slapped her hand over her mouth, shaking. "How much do you need? We'll cover it, you can pay us back whenever, no matter how long it takes."

"You can't help Rach, it is too much." Millie shook her head.

"Name it." Rachel oozed confidence, something Millie had always envied her for.

"Two million dollars." Out loud, the amount seemed insurmountable. "It covers everything. The house and contents, the land, all the machinery, and the stock. I'll lose everything."

"Millie, I don't know what to say."

"All those things we had, everything we had ever wanted, we got. The horses, musical instruments we never learnt to play, a birthday event every year. I never even thought about where the money was coming from, it never even occurred to me. I just presumed that he had the money, that we were lucky, luckier than others in town, who we saw struggle each year. When I think about everything that he did for us, or got for us, or allowed us to experience, I just feel ill."

"What did Josh say?"

"I haven't spoken to him yet; he is on a training mission and not contactable until the end of the month."

"Oh Millie, we'll figure something out, we have to."

"I don't think that I have that many options, to be honest with you Rach. I could sell off the land in parcels, and just leave the acre around the house for Josh and I. I could sell off anything that we have of value, all my grandfather's antique furniture and paintings, the farming equipment and leftover stock, the horses too. But even then, I am not sure we would be able to raise enough in such a short amount of time. When I spoke to the bank manager today, I asked him for an extension, and he turned me down flat. He wants his money."

"I'll talk to mum and dad tonight; we'll ask around town. There must be something we can do, a charity concert or auction or fundraising event of some kind."

When Millie finally left Rachel's coffee shop, there was a slight chill in the air, and the sun was just dipping below the horizon. Nothing had been sorted out, but just talking to Rachel had made Millie feel a whole lot better. As she shifted her Ute into gear and pulled out of the parking lot, Millie gazed out of the window at all of the happy holidaymakers, without a care in the world. She had been overly confident in her abilities, thinking that she could turn her grandfather's property into a boutique wedding destination that brides would vie for, and now she was paying the price. Two million dollars was a lot of money, money that Millie could hardly imagine. Two million dollars was more money than she and Josh would earn, collectively, in their entire lives, she was sure of it. She sighed heavily. She didn't know anyone who had that kind of money. Well, unless you count the Marsden family, which Millie most certainly did not!

The Marsden family had been a part of Maitland since the year dot, Millie wasn't sure how many generations of their family had worked their land. They were revered around here, treated like royalty. Millie quite liked June Marsden and her husband Robert, they were kind to all they met. Their sons, however, were an entirely different matter. Jack Marsden was the youngest, Millie's age. She wasn't particularly close with him, as far as Millie knew, he was a pretty high flyer in Sydney, he hardly ever returned home to Maitland. Then there was Samuel, the elder brother. The same age as Josh, they had taken to each other the same way Rachel had taken to Millie. Samuel and Josh had been inseparable, much to Millie's chagrin. She had never liked Samuel, had always found him to be too sure of himself, too arrogant to be worthy of her time. He had been a firm friend to Josh though, was still his closest friend, and for that, Millie would always welcome him with politeness, even if they would never be close themselves.

As Millie continued her drive back to her grandfather's property, for in her head that is what it would always be, his, regardless of whose name was on the title deed, a seed of thought began to take shape. Once home, Millie slipped out of her going-out-in-public-and-need-to-make-a-good-impression-outfit, and into her everyday house clothes of leggings and a tee-shirt. Millie had never been one for fuss and bother, much preferring comfort over any form of style. Millie made herself a strong cup of coffee and took it through to the lounge room. She lit a fire in the fireplace, although it really was far too warm to need one, Millie found the flickering flames mesmerising and relaxing. She picked up a notebook and pen and started to jot down her idea. It was crazy really, maybe even bordering on insane. If it went badly, she would be laughed out of the house, she would never be able to look them in the eye again, would in all likelihood, need to move away from Maitland forever. Not that there would be a reason to stay, if this plan didn't work, she wouldn't have anywhere to stay, no place to call home, no venue to run her business, Blush Wedding Designs. She also ran the very real possibility of damaging her relationship with her brother.

She looked down at the paper in front of her. It was a major risk, she knew that. She had nothing to offer, yet everything to gain. This plan had to work, it had to, she could not fail at this, it was just far too important. Millie choked down her pride and nodded firmly, her mind made up. She would do it. First thing tomorrow morning she would go and ask to speak with him, she would beg if she had to, although she really hoped that she would not need to resort to such a tactic. If by some miracle, she did manage to raise enough money, or to borrow enough money, to cover her grandfather's bank loan, Millie still had the teensy weensy issue of how she would then manage to pay that loan back. A problem for another day, Millie decided, downing her remaining coffee in a single mouthful and standing. Right now, there were chores to be done before bed, and she would need to get a good night's sleep she was hoping to be able to pull off her audacious plan tomorrow morning. She would need time to prepare, to look the part. It would not be at all advantageous for her to go begging in her house clothes, evidence of a sleepless night showing beneath her eyes.

No, Millie squared her shoulders as she headed for the barn, tomorrow she would look as if she were dripping in money, no matter how long it took her to get ready in the morning. She would wear her best outfit, the one usually reserved for weddings. Tomorrow, it would be her battle armour. She was not going to lose her grandfather's farm, not without a fight.

CHAPTER TWO

Sam spun into his driveway, gravel spewing from beneath his tyres. He came to an abrupt halt beside the main house, slamming his car door and heading towards the backdoor. Brunch with his parents always made him edgy, he needed a stiff drink. A slight movement to his left brought him up short and he paused, turning slightly, irritation lining his face at the sight of a woman, her back to him, peering into the guest house.

"Can I help you?" Sam frowned, he wasn't expecting any guests, unless his mother had started her quest to have him married off early this year. He stifled a groan, changing course to stride towards the stranger. "This is private property, and you are trespassing." The stranger turned, blue eyes clashing with green, recognition flaring in his eyes. "Millie."

"Hello Samuel." Her lips thinned out, pressing together, she looked as comfortable here as he imagined that she would look swimming with sharks. The silence stretched on between them, with Millie standing there looking up at him expectantly.

"Would you like to come in? Or perhaps you would rather I left you alone so that you could continue your snooping in peace?" Sam turned on his heel and headed back to the house.

"I wasn't snooping." Millie caught up with him at the front door, cheeks pink from trying to catch up with him. Or perhaps she was lying? Sam never knew with Millie; he didn't know her well enough to know her tells yet. He did know that Josh, her brother, was devoted to her, and given their history, it was not at all surprising to Sam. When Josh had joined the army, he had made Sam promise to look out for Millie, to look after her should anything ever happen to him. He had agreed without question, Josh was his closest friend, he would never have refused. If the tables had been turned, he knew Josh would be there for his brother and parents. He wondered idly if Millie knew of their agreement. He shot her a sideways glance and decided that no, she probably did not know. One thing he knew for sure about Millie was that she was fiercely outspoken, if she had known of their agreement, he would have seen her long before now, her guns blazing. Which is what made her visit here today so intriguing.

"No? Then what were you doing?"

"I was looking for you, actually, but there was no answer when I knocked at the door. I thought that you might have been in the guest house, I remember it used to be your office."

"No," Sam nodded in agreeance, "I was up at my parents' house for brunch, we do it every Saturday, it has become something of a tradition." Not to mention a great chance for his mother to remind him, yet again, that he is single, and the names of all of the available women in town.

"Is something wrong with Josh?" Sam led Millie through to the kitchen, gesturing towards the coffee maker perched on the countertop. "Coffee?"

"No, thank you." Millie had stopped just inside the kitchen door. "Josh is fine, he's currently stationed in Darwin," the pride in her voice was evident. "Did he tell you? He is taking part in a joint operation task force with the United States army. He should be back home at the end of the month."

"So, tell me then Millie," Sam leant against the kitchen bench, arms crossed over his chest, and looked at Millie, "just why exactly are you here today?"

"I...I came to ask you for a favour, Samuel, I don't have anyone else to ask."

"Really?" He quirked an eyebrow, of all the things he thought Millie might be here for, asking him for help was not one of them. As far as he could remember, Millie had never asked for help, from anyone, ever. Not even when her grandfather had died and the town had rallied around, it had been her friend, Rachel, who had organised a roster of people to deliver food and help out with the property, not Millie. Not that anyone would have refused, Millie's grandfather had been a well-respected and much-loved member of Maitland, it was their privilege to help his grandchildren after his passing.

"I have come to ask you for a loan." She squared her shoulders, her gaze not quite meeting his.

"Go on, I'm listening." Now, this was interesting.

"I have written up a proposal of sorts, obviously I would expect you to look over it and to make any alterations that you require," she absently waved a stack of papers in his direction. "I need to borrow two million dollars, I'm desperate!" She blurted out.

"Two million dollars!" Sam was floored, why on earth did Millie need that amount of money? "What kind of trouble are you in Millie?"

"I'm not in trouble, not really. It's the farm, I found out yesterday that my grandfather had taken out a second mortgage on the property, and that has now come due. I can't lose that farm Samuel," Millie cleared her throat, "I just can't."

"Two million dollars is a lot of money Millie."

"I know." He had to strain to hear her voice. "If there was any other way Samuel I wouldn't be here, you know that. I'm desperate. The bank won't extend the loan, and there is no way that I have that kind of money laying around. I don't have anybody else who can help me Samuel, you're the only one I know who has that kind of money. I'm not asking for me, I'm asking you to lend me the money for Josh. I can't give you anything for collateral, everything we have is tied up in the property, but I will pay you back Samuel, I promise, even if it takes me the rest of my life." Sam looked at Millie, really looked at her. The navy and white polka dot fit and flare dress that she wore looked stunning on her, it emphasised her delicious curves in all the right places. She had swept her auburn hair up into a knot on top of her head, a few tendrils had worked loose, falling down to frame her face, classically beautiful. He doubted that she even knew, even as a child Millie was less concerned with her appearance and more concerned with inner beauty. Why wasn't she married yet? Sam knew that the local bachelors had noticed her, had tried to get her attention, but so far none had succeeded.

"What is in it for me Millie, if I lend you the money you need, apart from the loan being repaid of course?"

Sam watched as Millie's face transformed, the nervousness gone, replaced with hope, liquid sunshine spilling from her eyes.

"Anything you want." She didn't even need to think about her answer.

"Anything Millie, are you sure about that?" He saw a slight shudder run through her, was it fear? Anticipation? He wished that he knew.

"I'm sure." Her voice didn't waver at all, Sam was impressed, she was certainly committed to her cause.

"So let me get this right." Sam pushed himself away from the kitchen bench and stalked towards Millie, slowly, deliberately, until they were standing toe to toe, keeping his voice dangerously low. "If I lend you two million dollars, in return you will give me anything that I want? Anything at all?" His gaze lingered on her lips; he had an overwhelming urge to kiss her right now. If she wasn't his best friend's sister, he would have her against the wall, would be claiming her with his mouth.

"I might not like you that much Samuel, but I'm not stupid. The reason you can have anything you want is because I trust you. You would never hurt me; Josh means too much to you for that to ever happen." She was right and yet Sam still did not move.
"Two million dollars." Sam mused.
"By the end of the month."
"That's three weeks."
"I know."
"Have you told Josh about this? Does he know that the property is in danger, that you need the money, just how you pan to get the money?"
"No, and he can't ever find out. I don't want him to worry, not if I can fix it."

"For once, that is something that we can agree on." Sam stepped back, taking Millie's paperwork from her, he crossed the room to the dining table and sat, spreading the papers out in front of him.

The proposal was good, and if they both signed it in from of a lawyer, Sam was confident that it would be legal. He was starting to wonder if Millie had meant what she had said, would she really give him anything, to save her property? He decided to find out.

"Have you met my mother, Millie?"

"Yes, many times, she's very nice." Millie joined him, choosing the chair farthest from his. She was, Sam knew that. He knew he was lucky to have her, despite her crazy matchmaking attempts.

"She wants me married off with a brood of children."

"Is that such a dreadful thing?" Millie shrugged, Sam guessed that for her, it would be a dream life.

"For other people? No, not at all."

"For you?"

"Yes." He looked her straight in the eye. "I don't intend to get married Millie; it was never in my life plan. My mother on the other hand..." he trailed off.

"Let me guess, she wants to see you married, a dozen cute kids calling her Grandma?"

"Cute?" He smiled at her, she thought he was cute.

"I assumed that your wife would be pretty." She smirked at him. Ouch!

"I have a counter-proposal."

"I'm listening." She leant forward, propping her elbows on the table in front of her.

"Marry me." He stated simply.

"I beg your pardon?!"

"Marry me. You need two million dollars and I need a wife."

"For what exactly? Surely you can go into Sydney and hook up anytime you like? You literally just told me that you never intended to marry."

"Not for that Millie, yeesh!"

"Seriously. You propose to me and then insult me, no wonder your mum thinks you need help finding a wife." Sam laughed; he had forgotten what a wildcard Millie could be.

"I'm curious, are you annoyed with me for not wanting to be physical with you, or are you annoyed because you wanted to turn me down first?" He held his hands up in surrender. "Seriously Millie, you're my best friend's kid sister. You were right before, I would never do anything to hurt you, and a fling would hurt you. Not at first, but later. This is business only, I give you my word. All I need is a wife for Christmas. That's all. Two weeks. If you agree to do this for me, to be my fiancé for two weeks, then I will give you the money you need Millie. You have my word."

"So, we would just be pretending right, I don't actually have to marry you?"

"No, but it does need to be believable Millie."

"Why do you need a wife so badly?"

"Honestly?"

"That would probably be best, don't you think? If I am going to be your pretend fiancé, I should probably know if there are any flames out there gunning for me."

"No flames, I assure you. At least none that I know of. It's for mum actually, think of it as a Christmas gift if you like."

"A Christmas gift? An engagement and then presumably a public break up of some kind. I know that I don't know your mum that well Samuel, but that does not sound like the type of

Christmas present that anybody would actually want. Why are you trying to fool her? Why don't you just tell her the truth, that you don't want to get married?"

"My parents have been married for forty years, and together even longer, since they first met in primary school. She wants the same thing for my brother and I, a loving, stable, forever type of love."

"I can understand that."

"You probably see it a lot, Josh tells me that your wedding planner business is really taking off."

"He's being kind, or maybe hopeful. The truth is, even without this surprise mortgage my grandfather hid from us, I am not sure how much longer I can afford to keep Blush Wedding Designs afloat. I just thought that it was such a novel idea, a boutique wedding venue, perfect scenery, space for a reception, as well as the honeymoon cottage, but the truth is, as creative as I am in planning a wedding, I am not particularly good at the other aspects of running a business, you know, the important parts, like advertising, selling myself to clients, I hate that, talking about myself, I always get so very self-conscious. Truthfully, I am starting to see that I do not make a very good business owner. I'll save the property, for Josh and I, but as far as my business is concerned, I am not sure I will manage to continue it for very much longer."

"I'm sorry Millie, I didn't realise. Why didn't you come to me?"

"Are you serious?"

"Why not?" Sam shrugged. "In case you didn't know, I do own one of the most prestigious advertising firms in the country. I'd be happy to sit down with you and see if we can work out a plan."

"Huh. Okay then, thank you. I didn't ask you Samuel because I didn't think you would say yes. We don't know each other, outside of Josh, why would you care." Millie shrugged.

"Regardless, you could have come to me. Anytime."

"Noted."

"So, will you do it, Millie? Two weeks as my fiancé for two million dollars?"

"What would it involve exactly?"

"I would expect you to meet my parents obviously, that is the main reason for the deception. I want you to help me convince them that we are in fact a happily engaged couple." Sam passed her contract back to her.

"Mum always has a few Christmas events planned, dinners and parties and the like, so I would expect you to accompany me to those. Basically, Millie, just be yourself, that's all. I don't expect any public displays of affection, Millie, but we will need to at least look comfortable in each other's presence, so maybe hold off on all of the withering glances you throw my way."

"Puh-leeze, I don't throw you withering glances."

"You used to."

"I did." She shot him a long look, holding his gaze. "I'm sorry, I just never really took to you, I don't know if it was because you were Josh's friend, or because of your self-arrogance, but I never really gave you that much time."

"Maybe you should have."

"Maybe you're right."

"Well, what do you say Millie? Will you marry me?"

CHAPTER THREE

Millie looked at Samuel closely, trying to decide if she could trust him or not. On one hand, she really was desperate, on the other, lying to his mother, about something as important as an engagement, did not sit right with Millie.

"Why lie to your mum? Why not just tell her the truth?"

"Believe me, I've tried. Mum doesn't want to hear it, she is convinced that all I need to do is just meet the right person, and then my views will change, and I will hurry down the aisle."

"Maybe she is right?"

"I'm thirty-one years old Millie, I think I know my mind by now."

"Maybe, maybe not." She eyed him sceptically.

"You think I'll suddenly change my mind? Are you a romantic Millie?"

"I'm a wedding planner Samuel, of course, I'm a romantic. But I am also a realist."

"You aren't comfortable lying."

"No," Millie admitted.

"And yet you intend to lie to Josh."

"It's different."

"How?"

"This lie isn't going to hurt him." Millie defended. "I intend to tell him the truth anyway, once I have solved the problem and he gets back home." He was right, she had to concede. She was lying to her brother. How was it any different?

"Okay, fair enough. Would it make you feel better if I told you that I also intended to tell my mother the truth?"

"Really?"

"Of course, one day."

"When?" Millie pushed.

"Before next Christmas I suppose, I can't very well expect you to play my fake fiancé every year, can I. Besides, you would send me broke." He smiled at her, and she chuckled.

"Touché. Although," she paused, appearing to consider her next words carefully, "it would be a rather unique way to earn a living. I could get used to only working two weeks a year."

"As if! You are always on the go; I think this is the longest time that you have ever sat still."

"True. Oh well, a girl can dream, can't she?"

"Is that what you dream about Millie? Having money? Being a lady of leisure?"

"No."

"What do you dream of then?"

"I dream of having the things that most people take for granted. A family, people who love me and support me and who want the best for me. A nice house, a job that fulfils me. A husband, someone to share life's ups and downs with, someone who I can always turn to, no matter what. Maybe, if I am lucky, a family of my own, children, a dog."

"Normal, average stuff."

"There's nothing wrong with average Samuel, not everybody in this world wants millions of dollars and private jets."

"I know. It sounds like a nice life Millie; I hope that you get it one day."

"What about you Samuel? What is it that you dream of when you are not busy trying to foil your mother's matchmaking attempts?"

"I don't really have any future dreams. For now, keeping my mother off my back is enough of a goal."

"And for that, you need my help."

"It does seem like the perfect solution, wouldn't you agree? To be honest, it was never something that I would have considered on my own, but your contract gave me the idea. You need money, and I need a wife, or more specifically, a fiancé for Christmas."

"I am tempted Samuel, I won't lie, it is a very attractive offer, I just don't know if it is something that I can do."

"I understand."

"How would it work exactly?"

"Well, as I said, I would expect you to meet my parents obviously, and to help me convince them that we are in fact a happily engaged couple. Attend a few Christmas events, dinners and parties and the like."

"What about everything else, all the ancillary things, have you thought about how they would work?"

"Such as...?"

"Such as the fact that no one in the town has ever seen us together, as a couple I mean, I know they have seen us plenty of times when we have had Josh with us, but there is no way any of those times could ever be considered a date."

"Fair point."

"Then of course there are your parents, won't they find it a bit odd that the first time they are meeting me is when you are announcing our engagement?"

"We'll think of something to tell them Millie, don't worry."

"Correction, you will think of something to tell them. Besides, that still leaves the most obvious issue of all." Millie looked pointedly at Samuel.

"You're talking about Josh?"

"Of course, I'm talking about Josh! Aren't you in the least bit concerned about what he would think? About what anybody would think for that matter? This is a small town, Samuel, how on earth do you think we can possibly get away with this?"

"No one needs to know. We'll simply tell those closest to us, if we go over our story it will be believable. You are not the only one who is desperate Millie."

"We would need ground rules."

"Naturally."

"And a ring."

"Obviously." He smiled at her, a dimple showing on his cheek. "Any particular size Millie? Or colour?"

"What?"
"The ring?"

"Seriously?" Sam nodded. "Well, get whatever type you want, it is of no consequence for me. You're the one who is going to have to try to return it or sell it after Christmas."

"You honestly don't care?"

"Why would I?" Millie shrugged. "To be honest, I don't really see the point of an engagement ring, apart from telling the world how much money you have to spend on a single piece of jewellery."

"Are you serious?"

"Does that surprise you?"

"Yes. Most women can't wait to get a shiny bauble on their ring finger."

"Well Samuel, I am not like most women."

"No, you're not." Was that admiration in his voice?

"I just think that if you love someone, enough to want a forever with them, then a ring shouldn't matter. I mean, why are you marrying? Is it for the wedding or the marriage?"

"Wait here." Sam stood and left the room, leaving Millie sitting at the table, contemplating. "Here." He dropped a ring box onto the table in front of her.

"What's this?" Millie shot him a questioning look.

"Open it and see."

"Samuel, this is an engagement ring. Where on earth did you get this from? Oh, good grief! Please tell me that this is not from some failed relationship, a cursed ring." Millie joked. "Seriously, Samuel, this is a stunner! Where did you get it?" Millie had never seen anything quite as exquisite before in her life.

"That is an original icy white cushion cut diamond from the early twentieth century. It weighs over five and a half carts."

"It's ravishing!"

"I'm glad you like it, it was my grandmother's, that's why I have it, I inherited it, it has been sitting in my safe ever since. Well, what are you waiting for? Try it on."

Millie slipped the ring from the box and turned it over in her hands. It really was ravishing. It glittered and shone in the light, throwing out some serious sparkles. Mounted on platinum, with pave diamonds inlaid into the band, the single square diamond was flawless. A truly majestic and impressive showstopper. She drew the ring out of its box and slipped it onto her finger. It fit snugly against her skin, something that she was relieved about, it meant that there was less of a chance that she would accidentally lose it. She held her hand out in front of her, admiring the way the ring looked on her hand.

"This is crazy, it must be an antique."

"Probably, it is valued at over one hundred and eighty-eight thousand dollars."

"What?!" Millie ripped the ring off her finger and stuffed it back into the box. "Are you insane? I can't wear that!"

"Of course, you can Millie, it's just a bauble, isn't that what you said?"

"That was different, and you know it. That was said in the abstract, but this," she held out the ring box, "this is a family heirloom Samuel."

"Which my mother would expect to see on the finger of my fiancé." Samuel pushed the box back towards Millie. "Put it back on, it looks good on your finger."

"Well...Don't get used to it. When Christmas is over it is going back into the box." She slipped the ring back onto her finger.

"And back into the safe," Sam replied. "So, you'll do it, Millie? You'll be my fiancé?"

"I have three conditions."

"Name them."

"Number one, under no circumstances whatsoever can Josh ever know about this agreement of ours. Ever. Not even years from now. It's a dealbreaker."

"Agreed."

"Number two, I won't be blown off Samuel, I mean it. When this deal is over, we both still need to live here, I don't want people shooting me daggers with their eyes, or worse, pity glances."

"We'll part as friends. What's the third condition?"

"I won't change myself for you, not even for a scam engagement. I'll dress up when I need to, in my own clothes, but I won't change who I am or what I believe in."

"I would never expect you to change, for anyone."

"Good."

"Now, I also have conditions."

"Uh oh, let's hear them then."

"You need to stop calling me Samuel, everyone calls me Sam, it will look weird if you, the woman who supposedly loves me, calls me by my full name that not even my mother uses."

"Okay, anything else?"

"You need to spend some time here, looking around, getting familiar with the layout. I host a Christmas party here each year, and I don't want people wondering why you don't know where the kitchen is."

"Fair enough."

"I'll arrange for some photographs to be taken of the two of us and put up around the house. Your house too, just in case my mother pays you a surprise visit."

"You think she would?"

"Maybe, she most likely won't let you out of her sight until we wed." He joked.

"Anything else?"

"No."

"In that case Samuel...Sam," she corrected herself, "you have yourself a deal." She held out her hand for him to shake. "Now, let's talk logistics."

Thirty minutes later Millie was sitting on the back porch of Samuel's house, notepad in hand, furiously taking notes. It turned out that agreeing to be Sam's fiancé was more work than Millie had thought. Her notepad was full of a long list of events and occasions that Millie would be expected to attend with Sam, she would certainly have a full calendar this holiday season. Millie was exhausted by the time that she finally got home, an accomplished type of exhausted. She would save this property, of that she was now certain, there was no reason that she would fail. Sam had told her that he would deposit the money straight into the bank in plenty of time to cover the loan before it came due, and she trusted him. He might be arrogant and overly self-confident, but he was also loyal and honest. And, her inner voice reminded her, as sexy as sin. Not that she would ever think about that, the last thing she needed was to start developing any type of real feelings towards him, she already had enough complications in her life without adding to them.

CHAPTER FOUR

Millie stood in front of her bedroom mirror peering at her reflection. It had been two days, two days full of butterflies in her stomach, two days since she and Sam had made their agreement. Tonight would be their first outing together, the first time that she and Sam told anybody of their engagement. Millie was nervous. Although she had gone over the story again and again and again in her head, Millie was still nervous that she would get it wrong, that Sam's mother would see right through their ruse. Millie could not let that happen, Sam was counting on her, he needed her. Well, for this anyway. In most other aspects of his life, Sam Marsden needed no one but himself. Millie had put her engagement ring on already, she wanted to get the feel for wearing it, she didn't want to be caught repeatedly fiddling with it or adjusting it. She wanted to forget it was even there. With a final glance at her reflection, Millie turned and left the room, she had a long day ahead of her and she needed to keep herself busy.

Millie unhitched the gate and headed for the far pasture. She was never really a farm girl in the traditional sense, she had no desire to brand cattle or harvest crops, but she did enjoy the wide-open spaces. Millie liked keeping chickens for fresh eggs, and she had horses for riding and competing, but otherwise, the paddock was for wandering in, and for daydreams among the wildflowers. Millie crossed to the far side of the paddock where an aging apple tree bowed to the ground. She had loved sitting here as a teenager, munching on the apples while her nose was in a book. She was starting to feel a little stir crazy, she had been housebound for too long. Granted, it had only been two days, but it had felt like eons. She and Sam had decided that until they had seen his mother and announced their engagement, Millie should remain out of town, just in case she ran into anybody she knew, which was laughable really, as she knew everybody in town. It seemed grossly unfair to Millie, but she could understand where Sam was coming from, after all, it was Millie who was wearing the engagement ring, not Sam. Millie had spoken to Rachel several times a day on the telephone and had so far managed to dissuade her from coming out to the property to see her, but Millie knew that Rachel was starting to get suspicious.

Millie absently picked some stray wildflowers, tucking the makeshift posey up in her hair. She would call Rachel when she got back to the house, she would ask her over for lunch tomorrow, Millie had a feeling that she would want to discuss tonight's dinner with Rachel, would need to debrief with someone, confess her crazy plan to her friend. She knew Rachel would support her, no matter what, and Millie would appreciate having someone in her corner to keep her sane and focused on the end goal. Millie wasn't sure how long she walked for, she crossed through paddock fences and walked until the air-cooled around her. With a sigh Millie turned back towards the house, a scream renting the air as she came face to face with Sam, stumbling back in surprise, tripping over a hidden rock and falling to the ground, landing in a patch of prickles.

"Ouch! Good grief Sam, you nearly gave me a heart attack!"

"I'm sorry Millie, here," Sam reached down to pull her to her feet, "let me help you."

"What are you doing here?" Millie brushed some loose dirt and leaves off of her pants. "Apart from scaring me of course," she joked.

"I had some time, I thought that I would come and pick you up early, you know," he shrugged, "for dinner with my parents. You weren't up at the house, by the way, you need to start locking your doors, I figured you would have gone to the apple tree." He smiled. "You always loved that tree. I saw you over here and decided to come to meet you. I really thought that you would have seen me coming."

"Obviously not. You scared me half to death, don't do that again."

"I'll try hard not to, although you have to admit, it was pretty funny, seeing you jump like that."

"Hilarious. Come on, let's go back to the house, I had better get ready, at this rate we will be lucky to be on time, let alone be early." They walked in peace, comfortable enough not to need to fill the silence. "Make yourself at home," Millie offered once they had reached the house, "I'm going to go and take a shower."

Millie stood under the jets of steaming hot water, letting it wash away her worries. Adding an ensuite to her bedroom had been her one big splurge after inheriting her grandfather's property. She had based it loosely on a hotel one might find in a five-star hotel, complete with a separate couple's shower, and a sunken bath built into a bay window. The bath overlooked the private back courtyard and was one of Millie's favourite places. Not that she had time to really sit and enjoy it today, she needed to get ready to meet her mother-in-law. The thought made her snicker, the idea that she would have a mother-in-law. Maybe one day. Millie shut off the water and stepped out of the shower. She padded through to her bedroom and opened her wardrobe, rifling around inside until she found what she was looking for, a sea green, knee-length, halter top party dress. One of her favourite dresses, Millie had only worn it once before and she was looking forward to the chance to wear it again. She paired it with a pair of strappy green high heels, a simple gold tennis bracelet, and a pair of gold knot earrings. A slick of dusk pink colour on her lips and a spritz of her favourite scent and she was ready to return to Sam.

A low appreciative wolf whistle greeted Millie as she stepped into the loungeroom, and she gave a slow turn.

"Millie, where on earth have you been hiding? You look smoking hot in that dress!"

"Thank you." Millie couldn't hide the blush that was creeping up her neck, had never been able to, a curse she blamed entirely on the colour of her hair.

"Do you need a jacket? Mum likes to have dessert out on the patio, she claims the view is better, but I think it is her attempt at getting dad to admit that he likes an after-dinner cigar."

"I'm sure I will be fine; the nights are still balmy enough for now. Besides," Millie shot Sam a sideways glance, "you could always be a gentleman and offer me your jacket you know."

"Maybe I will." She could feel his eyes on her as she headed towards the front door, fissures of excitement shot down her spine and she shook her head to dispel the tingling. This was a ruse, she reminded herself. She had been single for way too long if she was starting to feel attracted to Sam, of that she was certain.

Sam's parents' house was imposing, there really was no other word that would adequately describe it. Designed after the imposing Georgian structures commonly found on plantations, it was monolithic in size, fronted by a circular driveway complete with an ornamental fountain taking centre stage. A columned verandah wrapped around the ground floor, and from what Millie could see, there were wraparound verandahs on the first and second levels as well.

"Oh, wow." Was all that she could manage at first glance.

"And just think, this was my mother being discreet." Sam joked, parking the car in one of the dozen undercover carports. "Wait here," he directed. Millie watched as Sam got out and made his way around to her door, opening it for her and offering her his hand. "Take my hand Millie", he added when she hesitated. Drawing in a deep breath, Millie took Sam's hand and stepped out from the car. "Remember to smile Millie," his voice was low, barely a whisper, "you're supposed to be happy remember? I'm the man of your dreams."

Sam led Millie up the driveway to the front door, currently framing two people, a couple, his parents. His father had his arm slung around his mother's shoulders, warm, open smiles on both their faces.

"Mum, Dad, I want you to meet Millie, my fiancé." Sam made the introductions. The quick gasp from his mother was a surprise, Millie had presumed that Sam had already told his parents of their engagement, it had never occurred to her that this would be the first time that they were hearing about it.

"Millie! Welcome, I'm Kathy, it is so nice to meet you." Sam's mother was the first to respond, stepping forward and embracing Millie in a tight hug, before releasing her to embrace her son.

"Millie, I'm John, welcome to the family. I can't believe that Sam has finally proposed, after all these years, I'm just so happy for both of you." Millie hoped that her surprise didn't show, she made a mental note to ask Sam about his father's comment later.

"I'm so happy for both of you, I can't believe you're engaged! Sam, I never thought it was ever going to happen, I thought I would miss out on being a grandmother altogether. Millie, I'm so happy it's you, I always knew it, even when you were children, I always knew that there was something special about you." Kathy started to cry, happy tears coursing down her cheeks. Millie's eyes widened, embarrassment colouring her cheeks. That was the second time someone had mentioned that they were not at all surprised that she and Sam were engaged. What on earth was happening? Why would someone think that she and Sam were an ideal, obvious even, couple? What in their future had ever hinted that they would end up together? Was it simply the fact that Sam and Josh were inseparable? Or was it something else? Had she been too transparent, too obvious in her infatuation of him as a child? For a very brief period of around six weeks, Millie had considered herself to be in love with Sam. She had been seventeen, and while completely certain of her feelings, she had never spoken of them to anyone, not even to Rachel. Had she been less adept than she had thought in hiding her reaction to Sam?

Millie thought back, wondering who could possibly have noticed, and more importantly, who could have told Kathy and John, and for what reason. They would have to have known that Millie would never act on any leftover feelings for Sam, certainly not after all these years. Another more mortifying thought occurred to Millie. Did Sam know? Those six weeks had been torture for Millie, she had locked herself away in her room, simultaneously fantasising about Sam kissing her, and dreading it at the same time. She had been a shy, awkward teenager. Maybe that was what drew her to Sam? He was always there at every turn, shadowing Josh. They had returned home for semester break, more filled out, more fit than they had left. He had seemed mysterious, a dangerous mix of experience and risk, and so very, very off-limits. Millie had barely spoken three words to him all summer, so tongue-tied had she become around him. She knew he had found her abrupt, it was why he still thought that she simply tolerated him. It couldn't be further from the truth, not that she would ever, ever let him find that out for himself. That was one secret that she intended to take to her grave.

"Well, come in, come in, don't just keep her standing out there on the doorstep Sam." His mother ushered them through the door, rolling her eyes at her son as she did. "Your father is barbecuing tonight Sam, why don't you go out on the back patio with him and supervise, make sure he doesn't set anything on fire like last time. I'll take Millie on a tour of the house."

"He set something on fire?" Millie couldn't help but ask her curiosity piqued.

"John is a sweetheart and I love him to death, but honestly, there is a reason that he doesn't do the cooking. The last time he barbecued one of the steaks caught on fire, John attempted to put it out with a tea towel, naturally, it went up in flames, which in turn set my ferns alight, and spread to the gazebo curtains." Kathy shook her head at the memory. "By the time John and Sam had put the fire out the gazebo, along with most of the back patio, looked like some decrepit skeleton of its former self. Naturally, we have not let him forget it." Millie smiled along with Kathy. "Now," Kathy looked her up and down, "let's start upstairs, shall we?"

"You have such a beautiful house, Kathy." Millie loved looking through houses, loved seeing how they were all decorated, it was what had originally drawn her to wedding planning, the design element.

"Thank you, it has been a labour of love. John and I have been restoring this place since we first bought it, we were finally able to move in a couple of years ago. I think that this is my forever house.”

“I can understand why.”

“Millie? Mum?” Sam found them upstairs in one of the many lounge areas. “Dad says the steaks are done.” He slung his arm around Millie’s shoulders and drew her to his side. “Let’s go eat before he sets another fire.”

“That was absolutely delicious John.” Millie leant back in her chair on the patio, her dinner plate empty.

“Yeah dad, they were great. Especially without the charcoal taste.”

“Ha ha Sam, very funny.” John was clearly used to the family ribbing him about his fire incident.

“Really dear, you outdid yourself tonight.” Kathy placed her hand on John’s forearm. “Thank you.”

“Sam, shall we walk around the garden while your mum and Millie talk?” Sam winked at Millie, he was on to his dad, his walk always being code for a cigar.

“Sure dad,” Sam rose.

“Wait.” Kathy stopped them in their tracks. “Would anyone like some dessert? I made my famous pavlova.” A chorus of yeses followed her question, and Millie offered to help her clear the table and bring it out, the women leaving the men to their secret cigar.

CHAPTER FIVE

With dessert finished, the two couples sat outside in the twilight sharing conversation and making new memories.

"So, Millie, you're a party planner, is that right?"

"I'm a wedding planner."

"Don't undersell yourself, Millie." Sam smiled at her. "She owns Blush Wedding Designs mum."

"Oh! I read about you in the paper, I am yet to get out to your property though, maybe I could pop out and have a look?"

"Of course, any time."

"Oh, that's so romantic! A wedding planner, planning her own wedding. You must already know what your dream wedding is, do you?"

"To be honest Kathy," Millie shot Sam a sideways look, "I haven't given it much thought. I guess I have just been too busy planning other people's weddings."

"Oh, I love weddings! There is just something so romantic about them, bringing families together, uniting people." Kathy gave a wistful sigh. "It almost makes me want to do it all over again."

"Why don't you? Renewal vows are always a popular idea, I organized a dozen in the past few months."

"John, did you hear that?" Kathy turned to John, her eyes shining bright. "What do you think?"

"Kathy love, would you like to remarry me?"

"Yes."

"Then let's do it, after Sam and Millie's wedding, we don't want to upstage them."

"Of course not, that's a wonderful idea."

"Oh Kathy, John, you don't need-"

"Dad, mum, seriously-" Sam and Millie protested at once, pausing when they realized the other was speaking, laughing as they both stopped. "Please," Sam indicated, "you go first."

"I was just saying that Kathy and John don't need to wait for us, in fact, they shouldn't wait for us, they should go ahead and get remarried. After all, we haven't even set a date yet, it could be years before we walk down the aisle."

"I agree. Seriously mum, dad, we are not even at the date setting stage, who knows how long it will take us. The last thing I want is for you to have to wait for us."

"Are you sure Sam?"

"Yes." He all but screamed. Millie pressed her lips together and tried not to smile, relieved that Sam had it all under control. He must know how uncomfortable she was with the thought of his parents waiting to renew their vows until she and Sam had wed. They would have been waiting forever!

"It's so exciting! Will you help me plan it, Millie? Sometime in March maybe, or February."

"Sure, I'd love to." Their conversation was interrupted by the ringing of the telephone, John excusing himself to go and answer it, returning to hand the telephone to Kathy.

"Oh, my goodness, you'll never guess who that was."

"Who?" Sam bit.

"Ron and Barb, from next door. Their daughter, Belinda, is due to marry her fiancé Greg in ten days' time, only Barb and Ron have just received a telephone call from an accountant up in Sydney. It seems that their wedding planner was a fraudster, she's done a runner with nearly five million dollars of other people's money, including not only the deposit, but the balance of the account that Ron and Barb have paid her for Belinda's wedding. Barb is in a terrible state, as you can imagine, they have no idea what they're going to do, they have nearly five hundred guests set to arrive in the next few days, and no idea if there will even be a wedding at this stage." Kathy shook her head in disbelief. "They were so careful; they checked her references and everything. I guess you just can't trust some people. Those who are determined to defraud and scam will always find a way.

"Sadly, that's true, and it happens a lot more than one might expect within the wedding industry. Poor things, do you know if they had wedding insurance at all? If they did, then at least they might be able to get some of their deposits back from the venues, small comfort I know, but at least it will be something." It made Millie so mad, the charlatans within the wedding planning business. Quite often what was supposed to be the best day of someone's life was ruined by shonky vendors and inexperienced wedding planners. Usually, these so-called wedding planners were entirely self-taught, and most of them had a real attitude of 'how hard could it be?'. It frustrated Millie no end, planning a wedding was a lot more involved than simply slapping together a mixed CD, ordering some wine, and booking a celebrant. It was all the millions of little things that went into making that one day perfect for that particular couple, from ensuring that the bride had dental floss to fix any wedding dress disasters, to making sure that the miniature cameo that hung from the wedding bouquets matched the cameo motif that was used throughout the wedding stationery and table linens, to simply checking that the bride and groom had a packed picnic to take with them after they left the reception, being a wedding planner was not easy.

"Barb is going to take Belinda into Sydney tomorrow in the hopes that they will be able to find another wedding planner who can step in and save the day, literally." Kathy sipped her coffee thoughtfully. "Unless...I don't suppose that you would be free, would you Millie?"

"That's a great idea love." John chimed in, three faces turning to look at Millie expectantly.

"You said the wedding was in ten days, is that right?"

"Yes," Kathy confirmed.

"Depending on just how much there is still left to do, I might be able to help, but it would depend. I currently only have one client booked this Christmas season, but he is incredibly demanding." Millie shot Sam a sideways glance, enjoying the way his lips quirked up on one corner. "If I can fit Belinda and Greg's planning in around this particularly difficult client, then I would be happy to help plan their wedding."

"Oh goodness, I'm going to go and call Barb right this minute, she is going to be so excited!" Kathy left the room at a jog.

"Millie, this would be a huge coup if you were able to help Barb and Ron." Sam leant closer to Millie. "They are hugely connected in Sydney, they have a number of high profile, celebrity friends. This could be an amazing opportunity for you, and for Blush Wedding Designs."

"Well, don't count my chickens until they hatch," Millie warned him, "I haven't even met with Belinda and Greg yet to see if we are compatible to work together."

"True." Sam shot her a wicked grin. "And then there is your very important client, you know, the uber demanding one that you have this Christmas. Gosh, I hope you can work around him."

"Oh, I'm sure that I can. You see Sam, he's incredibly desperate, he's paying big bucks for my services, no one else will do. I guess he will just need to learn to share me or find somebody else to replace me, which I think he will find a near impossible task." Millie smiled sweetly at Sam. Two can play at this game.

"Millie dear," Kathy returned to the patio, telephone tucked against her shoulder, "Barb is absolutely thrilled! She wants to know if you are free to pop over first thing tomorrow morning to meet with her and Belinda?"

"Tomorrow morning will be fine, let her know that I can be out there any time after eight o'clock in the morning." Kathy put the telephone up to her ear and relayed the message.

"Okay, uh-huh, no, of course, yes, absolutely, thank you, yes, we are so happy, obviously you know, yes indeed, come for afternoon tea tomorrow, okay Barb, talk later." Kathy ended the call. "She's excited about meeting you

Millie, she and Belinda will be waiting for you at eight o'clock in the morning, she said to let you know that she will have a nice breakfast ready and waiting for you."

"That's very sweet, but she doesn't need to do that." Millie protested.

"It is her pleasure Millie dear, trust me. She can't wait to meet you; she is nearly as excited as me that the two of you are engaged. Oh dear, I hope I didn't overstep the line by telling her your happy news?"

"No mum, it's fine." Sam was quick to reassure.

"She is like family, and I was so happy to share the news with her. She is nearly as excited as I am at the news. In fact, Sam, she asked if you wanted to join them tomorrow morning as well, it has been ages since she saw you last."

"Well," he shot a look at Millie, "if I won't be in Millie's way mum, after all, it is a work function for her."

"You won't be in my way at all Sam, although I am not sure how exciting you will find it, all that talk of weddings and colour schemes." It wasn't unusual for Millie to present her proposal and visions to both the bride and the groom, as well as to the bride's parents on most occasions, but this would certainly be the first time that she took a date along with her.

"In that case, I would love to tag along and see Millie in action."

A sudden thought of seeing Sam in action had Millie shivering, surprise etching her features when Sam stood up and removed his jacket, draping it over Millie's shoulders.

"See," his voice was a low whisper in her ear, "I can be a gentleman." The second shiver that ran down her spine had nothing to do with the cold, and everything to do with the look that accompanied his words. Millie was sure that everyone on the patio must have noticed the sudden shift in the air, the thick emotions swirling around, but no one said anything.

"Will you two be okay to drive back into town, or did you want to stay here tonight? There is plenty of room." John offered.

"Thank you but no. If I'm going to pitch a proposal to Belinda and Barb first thing tomorrow morning, I am going to need access to my studio and my ideas books." Millie answered before Sam had a chance to. She didn't trust him to say no, and she didn't trust herself to be under the same roof as him all night long, not if she wanted to get any sleep that is. Besides, it was true, she did need to access her studio and ideas books.

Millie and Sam stayed for another cup of coffee, before reluctantly bidding goodnight and heading out to Sam's car shortly before midnight.

"I must say, Sam, that was actually fun. Your parents are delightful, seriously, why don't you just tell them the truth. I was mortified when your mum said that she had told Barb that you are engaged. You are going to have one hell of a clean-up to do after Christmas Sam, you do realise that, don't you?"

"You worry too much Millie, it will be fine, I promise." Sam opened her car door for her, waiting until she was tucked safely inside before closing it and moving to his side of the car. "I told you, I will take care of it, you have nothing to worry about."

"Just promise me that you will do it with kindness Sam. I like your parents, I don't want to cause them pain, even indirectly."

"I promise."

Sam turned the heater up to high, a relief to Millie, who was starting to shiver.

"You should have brought that jacket."

"As much as I hate to admit it, Sam, you are right." Millie smiled across at him in the half-light of the dashboard. "That was really nice of your mum, recommending me like that to her friends. She didn't need to do that."

"She knows that, she wanted to. Mum likes helping others in their ventures, she is the best cheerleader that I know."

"It is a great opportunity."

"It is." Millie could feel Sam's eyes on hers momentarily. "You can say no Millie, I don't want to you think that you have to say yes tomorrow. If we get there and what they want and what you can offer are two different things, then I want you to know that you can say no, you can turn them down. There will not be any hard feelings from anyone, I promise you."

"I've never pitched for someone with this kind of budget or guest list before, it is slightly intimidating, overwhelming even."

"If anyone can do it, Millie, it is you."

"You can't possibly know that Sam."

"Sure I can." There was no hesitation in his voice.

"How can you sound so completely certain, so confident? You have never seen my work before."

"You might not realise this Millie, but Josh sends me copies of everything that you do. Every time you are in a magazine article or newspaper column or some bride writes you a thank you note in the local paper, I get a copy. He is so proud of you Millie."

"I never realised that."

"Well, there you go. I know you can do an amazing job for Belinda and Greg because I have seen your work before. You have talent, that much is clear, but more importantly, far, far more importantly, you have a real knack for finding that one element that truly makes each wedding unique and individual."

Millie wasn't quite sure what to say to that, she had never been very good at accepting compliments and to be honest she wasn't sure if she had ever heard Sam give any.

"Would you like me to pick you up in the morning Millie? Or would you rather take your own car over to Belinda's?"

"Thank you, Sam, but I think I will drive myself over, there is somebody that I need to see afterwards."

"Rachel?"

"Yes."

"You're going to tell her, aren't you?" Millie didn't need to ask what Sam was referring to, she already knew.

"Yes. I need to tell somebody, Sam, I need to have somebody to talk things over with, and Rachel is the perfect choice, I trust her with my life, she would never tell a soul."

"I know."

The rest of the ride to Millie's house passed in silence and all too soon Sam was coming around to open her car door for her, taking her elbow and guiding her to the front door, waiting patiently as she unlocked the door and let herself in, switching on the lights as she did so.

"Lock the door behind me, Millie, I'll go once I hear the click."

"I will. Goodnight Sam, thank you for tonight, I had fun." Millie was surprised to realise that she actually meant the words that she was saying.

"Goodnight Millie, sweet dreams." True to his word, Millie didn't see Sam return to his car until after she had locked the door behind him. She watched his car travel down her driveway and out of sight, before rousing herself to get started on her proposal for tomorrow morning. As she slipped into bed hours later, her last thought before succumbing to sleep was that it really had been a lovely evening with Sam.

CHAPTER SIX

Millie had spent most of last night putting together a proposal that she hoped would suit Belinda and Greg. As she pulled up in front of Ron and Barb's house, there were two women waiting out on the front patio to greet her.

"Millie?"

"Hi, you must be Barb."

"Yes, welcome. This is my daughter Belinda." Barb indicated the woman standing next to her. "We are so grateful that you were able to come over, thank you."

"Honestly, it is my pleasure. Shall we get started?" Barb showed Millie into the house, Belinda following closely behind. "I have us set up in the lounge room, I hope that that is suitable?"

"That will be fine." Millie put her large bag on the lounge room coffee table, pulling out colour swatches and photograph books showcasing her previous work. "I went ahead and wrote up a proposal of sorts, now please bear in mind that all of these elements are interchangeable. Obviously, I wasn't sure what you had previously planned or hoped for, so please think of this as a guide only."

"I only take one wedding booking per day," Millie started, "that's why the bride and the bridal party have the entire day with which to get ready, take their photographs, and just enjoy the venue. As well as the private honeymoon cottage, I also have a newly built chapel, which seats one hundred guests, with standing room for a further sixty. There is a repositionable dance floor, and a simply gorgeous gazebo, which looks absolutely stunning in the evening all bedecked with hundreds of fairy lights. It is entirely up to you, but my packages include all linens and décor items, a menu sourced from local suppliers, guest favours, flowers, all sound and microphone equipment, as well as my presence on the wedding day as standard, just in case any issues should arise. As I said, I can also add well subtract items as required. I work with a great vendor who is able to supply bridal party items such as bathrobes, slippers, and wine glasses, all emblazoned with either the bride's name or the positions of the bridal party, such as bride's mother if that is something that you wish to have as well." Millie, Barb, and Belinda were interrupted by the arrival of Sam, along with two other men, who barb introduced as her husband Ron, and Belinda's fiancé, Greg. "It's lovely to meet you both. Were you able to recover any of your original deposits or funds already paid?"

"No." Belinda looked close to tears, and Millie wasn't surprised, she knew that weddings were not cheap, and given her lavish surroundings, she could only imagine how much money had already been spent on Belinda's wedding. "Our lawyer spoke with the liquidator, and they say it will be unlikely that we ever get any money back, even if they manage to catch her and prosecute her, chances are that the money will already be long gone."

"I'm really sorry to hear that."

"Thank you. Um," Belinda blushed, "Greg and I were wondering, how much do you charge for your services?" Millie really felt for the woman, what a horrible situation to be in.

"As it happens, I actually have your original date free, so if you would still like to get married on the twentieth of December, you may. As for my fees, outside of what you will need to pay the vendors, it will be free, consider my services a wedding gift to you both." There was a squeal, and Millie found herself wrapped in two strong arms as Belinda embraced her, tears rolling down her face.

"Millie, thank you, thank you, thank you! You have no idea how much this means to us." Millie smiled, she could imagine how much it meant, if Belinda's reaction was anything to go by. The rest of the afternoon passed in a blur of wedding talk, whispered hopes, and cups of tea. By the time Millie made her excuses, she was mentally exhausted. Waving goodbye to Belinda, Greg, Ron, and Barb, Millie walked out to her car, accompanied by Sam.

"That was a nice thing that you did in there Millie."

"You surprise me, Sam, I thought that you would lecture me on business versus charity."

"I'll let this one slide. Seriously, it was very sweet, you made her day."

"It was one way that I could help, and it costs me nothing to do so."

"Every time I think I know you; you go ahead and surprise me again."

"Good night Sam." Sam helped Millie into her car, closing the door behind her.

"Good night Millie." Sam stood there watching Millie drive away, he was still standing there when she turned the corner.

CHAPTER SEVEN

Millie looked out of her bedroom window and sighed. It had been four days since she had seen Sam, and while they spoke every day on the telephone, she was feeling out of sorts. Was it possible that she was missing him? Missing Sam? Annoyed at herself for her thoughts, she angrily rubbed a hand over her eyes. No doubt Sam would come and see her when he was ready, or rather, when he needed a date to some Christmas function, until then, she had work to do. Today Millie was hosting Belinda's kitchen tea, and there was still a lot of things that Millie needed to get set up. Showering quickly, Millie dressed in a pair of black silk work trousers, paired with an apricot-coloured ruffle neck cap-sleeved blouse, and black ballet flats, Millie's shoe of choice for every occasion. It wasn't that Millie couldn't appreciate a nice high heel, she could, and she knew that they had their purpose, just not for her. Millie had literally the worst coordination of anyone that she knew, and the last thing that she needed was to attempt to balance her body weight atop the very thin pole of a high heel spike. No, Millie stuck to ballet flats at all costs.

Millie drove her car as close to her front door as was possible, opening the boot and going inside, bringing box after box of party goodies out to place in the boot. She had bags of prizes for the games she had planned, decorations, signage and badges, and the floral arrangements that she had personally driven into Sydney for the day before. She was all set. Barb and Belinda had opted to host the wedding kitchen tea at their house, they were expecting close to sixty women, and the house offered a more intimate setting for Belinda and her guests. Millie loved hosting a bridal kitchen tea, it was a joy to be able to gather the bride's closest female family members and friends, to celebrate the bride-to-be as she moves into the next chapter of her life. Millie mentally went over her checklist as she drove across town to Barb and Belinda's house, she wanted to make sure that everything was perfect for Belinda today, she didn't want to leave anything to chance.

"Millie, good morning." Barb met her at the door, pulling her into a hug.

"Morning Barb, is Belinda up yet?"

"She's just in the shower as we speak. Do you need any help bringing your bags in?"

"Thank you, that would be great." With Barb's help, it only took two trips to carry all of Millie's bag into the kitchen and spread them out on top of the kitchen table. Millie started unpacking the bags onto the kitchen table, pausing when Belinda entered the room. "Belinda, you look beautiful!" Dressed in an apricot-coloured knee-length strapless peplum dress with sweetheart neckline, Belinda looked every bit the blushing bride. Hearing Millie's greeting, Barb entered the kitchen, her hand flying to her mouth, a gasp escaping, as she laid eyes on her daughter.

"Belinda." The single word was full of emotion, a single tear fell from Barb's eyes and raced down her cheek. Mother and daughter embraced tightly, before Barb gently pushed Belinda away, patting her on the arm. "Come now, we can't start crying now, or else we'll both be in tears all morning."

"Your mum's right, this will be an emotional day, for both of you, so take a moment if you need one. Just remember the most important thing, Belinda." Millie advised.

"What's that?"

"Everyone who will be joining us here today is doing so because of you. They don't care about what food you serve them, or what favours they win in the games, or even how the house is decorated. They only care about one thing. You. That is why they are here, because they love you and they want to celebrate and contribute to, your future and your happiness. And that," Millie passed Belinda the box of tissues sitting on the kitchen table, "is all that really matters, I promise you."

"Thank you," Belinda murmured from behind her tissue.

"Now, why don't you two lovely ladies go back upstairs and finish getting ready, if any guests start to arrive early, I shall direct them out onto the back patio, just as we planned, okay?" Belinda and Barb nodded to Millie and left, headed upstairs, arm in arm. Millie smiled, quite often the wedding events were more emotional for the bride's mother than for the bride herself.

Millie busied herself out on the back patio, making sure that all of the rented tables and chairs were arranged just as Belinda had wanted, the ten round white tables each surrounded by six white chairs, all framing a larger white table in the centre, where Millie had placed various sized vases of flowers, along with the four-tiered cake. There were more white tables placed off to the sides, a table to place the gifts on, tables of gorgeously arranged glasses and plates, a table holding name tags and party bags, and a long table for the buffet brunch that Millie was in the process of setting up. Millie had stuck to Belinda's colour scheme of apricot throughout the entire planning, including the buffet. The long table contained gorgeous vintage inspired tiered cake plates and platters, a stunning display of florals and apricots, offering up an array of treats such as miniature individual orange cakes and carrot pies, apricot crumbles and crème brulees. It was warm and inviting, and Millie knew that Belinda was going to love it! Barb and Belinda came back downstairs shortly before the first guests started to arrive, and Millie helped to position them into a receiving line, she knew that when the guests arrived the first thing that they would want to do would be to congratulate and speak with Belinda.

Once all of Belinda's guests had been seated, Millie stood up to speak.

"Good morning. I would just like to take this opportunity, on behalf of Barb and Belinda, to welcome everybody here today, and to thank you all for joining us in the celebration of Belinda and Greg's upcoming wedding. Today is a celebration of love and friendship, the perfect opportunity to spend time with Belinda, and to wish her well in her life ahead." Millie nodded for the servers to start rotating throughout the room with their trays, and took her seat at the bride's table, along with Barb, Belinda, Greg's mother, Greg's sister, Belinda's three bridesmaids, and all four grandmothers'. As the brunch got underway, Millie circulated amongst the guest tables, making sure that everyone was having fun, and that each of the guests had their copy of the crazy vows game in front of them. As they ate, Millie directed them to fill in their sheet of questions, that would help Belinda to write her own vows, the funnier the better. Once all of the sheets had been completed, Millie requested a volunteer to read out the results.

"I Belinda, take you Greg to be my husband." Belinda's future sister-in-law had stood up to read the sheets out, happiness radiating from her face. "You are my nineteenth true love, I will cherish and love you, today, tomorrow, for six weeks." The laughter around the room was loud, this game was popular with every wedding that Millie had ever hosted. "I will laugh with Mary and cry with Brenda, through good times and fluffy times, hard times and sparkly times. Whatever happens, Kathy will always be there." The game finished with a round of applause, Millie always liked to start the festivities off with this game as it was a no-pressure game that ladies of all ages could play, it was a great ice breaker and a way for both sides of the family to get to know each other if they didn't already. This was followed by a game of who am I, using the guests themselves as the celebrities their fellow guests had to guess. Wedding charades came next, followed by wedding Pictionary, with Millie making sure that two different tables were declared the winners. Millie knew from experience that everyone had a much better time if the winners of each game were always different tables, even if that meant that they had to be awarded points in a creative fashion!

"For this game, each person who wishes to play will need to stand up and share three stories about experiences they've had with the bride. Here's the catch," Millie smiled at the faces in front of her, "two stories must be true, and one must be false. After you have told us your three answers, everyone will vote on which one they think is the lie. If you guess correctly, you get a point. Easy. Now, who wants to go first?" Millie handed her microphone over to the first volunteer, heading over to the prize table to make sure her prizes were ready. Millie had two more games left to play, she had saved the best for last and wanted to make sure that every person left with a prize as well as their goodie bag. "Played like a scavenger hunt, the first person to hold up the item that I call out wins the point," Millie explained the rules of her next game, the handbag raid. As well as calling out standard items that you would expect to find in a woman's handbag, like tissues, lip balm, and a credit card, Millie also called out more random and risqué items, like pink sunglasses, a scratched DVD, and contraception. The handbag raid game was a huge hit, as it always was, and as always, Millie was surprised by just who had what in their bag, especially when it came to items like the g string.

"Ladies you have all been fantastic sports today, and I hope that you have had fun playing these games with Belinda and Barb. I have one last game for you all to enjoy before we move across to watch Belinda open her gifts, and this one was saved for last as Belinda wanted you all to enjoy every aspect of her kitchen tea, even the gift opening. So, without further ado, we are going to play pass the parcel, with a twist." Millie held up a large package for everyone to see. "On each wrapped layer is written a question and everyone here has to decide who it suits. Whoever you declare the winner gets the prize from the next layer of the parcel. There are enough gifts inside this parcel for everyone here, it is simply up to you to decide who it suits best. Are we ready?" At the guest's excited nods, Millie read out the first question. The questions were always fun, and generally included things such as who has the best painted toenails? Who is the tallest? Who has the longest hair? Who is wearing the most jewellery? Who has the highest heels? The questions went on and on until the parcel of prizes had passed through each pair of hands, and every guest there held a small trinket, in this case, a stunning apricot coloured teardrop shaped crystal that Belinda had requested be made into either a necklace, charm bracelet, or keyring, giving the ladies plenty of options. Millie did not doubt that the crystal was real, not an imitation if the bill was anything to go by.

After everyone had admired their prizes and finished up their brunch, Millie encouraged them all to turn their chairs, or even to move them if they wanted to, so that everyone would be able to see Belinda as she opened her gifts. Gift opening was not always something that Millie was privy to, a lot of her brides preferred opening their gifts in private with their groom after the wedding kitchen tea was finished, this way they didn't need to worry about their face giving away their true feelings, but Belinda and Barb were adamant. These were their closest friends, and they would treasure everything that they were given, no matter the cost or size, as they knew it had been given in love. Millie wished that all of her brides to be felt that way. Millie kept track of which guest gave which gift in her planner, she would pass it on to Barb later so that thank you notes could be written and sent. Belinda seemed genuinely delighted in her gifts, ranging from a coffee maker and cutlery set to a baking ware set and linen, and everything in between. This would be the first house that Belinda and Greg would share, both having lived with their parents until now, and her wedding registry had been full of house related items that they needed.

Belinda's last gift was the most special. When Millie had sent out the invitations, she had requested that each guest handwrite their favourite recipe and return it to Millie before the day of the kitchen tea, which they had all done. Millie had then taken those cherished recipes and had them scanned and collated, printing them into a stunning recipe book for Belinda to pore over in years to come. Kept secret from Belinda, Millie knew that this would be a truly unique gift! As she opened it, Belinda started to cry, holding it up for everyone else to see, going through it page by page and calling out the recipe and the giver. By the time Belinda had finished exclaiming and pouring over her gift, there wasn't a dry eye in the house. It had been a wonderful kitchen tea, as the last guest left, Millie started cleaning up, happy to help the hired staff, she knew that they were just as keen to get home as she was. While it had been a great day, it had also been a tiring one. Millie helped Belinda to carry all of her gifts inside and up to the spare room, which had currently been turned into wedding central, and then returned downstairs to make sure that everything had been put back to its original state. With the house and garden passing muster, Millie happily wrote a cheque out to the hired wait staff and saw them out.

Millie went on the hunt for Barb, finding her in the kitchen making herself a cup of tea. She smiled as Millie approached.

"Millie, thank you, today was wonderful."

"It was my pleasure, Barb." Millie sat on one of the kitchen bar stools. "I have the list for you, of who gave what gift, you said you wanted to send the thank you notes yourself."

"Yes, thank you, it is the least that we can do, everyone has been so kind to us, especially considering…" Barb trailed off.

"Well, it might not be the wedding that she had planned originally, but it will still be the most magical day of her life." Millie was quick to reassure Barb.

"I know it will dear, especially now that we have you to help us." After making sure that

Barb didn't need help with anything else, Millie packed away the last few remaining items into her car boot and headed for home, and what she hoped would be a nice long soak in her bathtub.

CHAPTER EIGHT

By the time that Millie finally got home and had finished unloading her car, she was completely exhausted. She wondered if she could justify going to bed before the sun had set. As she lay on the couch, her feet propped up on a pillow, considering this option, her telephone rang. She glared at the offending item, sitting on the kitchen table across the other side of the room, bleating at her. With a sigh, Millie stood up. She knew that she couldn't let it ring endlessly, it might be important, it might be Rachel or Josh.

"Hello."

"Millie? This is Kathy."

"Kathy, hi."

"I just wanted to call and let you know what a wonderful day it was today, everybody had so much fun, but more importantly, the emotion, the love in the room, the absolute joy, was palpable. It made me wistful. And it also got me thinking about you and Sam, and your big day. I was wondering, hoping actually, that she might be free to have lunch with me tomorrow.”

“Kathy, um, let me just pop you on hold for a moment and go and check my diary.” Millie muted Kathy before she could reply, dropping the telephone onto the table. This was not something that Millie had planned for. She had expected that any family interactions would occur with Sam present, not as a cosy one on one, and she wasn't quite sure how to handle Kathy’s request. Unable to talk it over with Sam, merely decided to go with her gut instinct. “Kathy, are you there? Sorry about the wait, as it happens, I am free all day tomorrow. I would love to join you for lunch, what time should I meet you?”

“Oh, that’s wonderful! Shall we say midday? There is a great little place in Maitland, on the Main Street, called The Daily Grind, do you know it?”

“I sure do, my best friend, Rachel, owns it.”

“Oh, I love that place. Shall we meet there? Maybe if your friend is free, she could join us?”

“Sure, it sounds like fun. I’ll see you there then.” Millie and Kathy chatted about generic things for a few more minutes before Millie ended the call.

Millie sent Sam a text message, letting him know that she was going to be having lunch with his mother tomorrow, and asking him to call her when he was free. Millie fixed herself a Turkey and salad sandwich for dinner, which she ate on the lounge in front of the television, as she binge watched a couple of episodes of her favourite television psychological crime show. When Sam still had not called her at eight o'clock at night, Millie shrugged and switched off her phone, taking herself upstairs and collapsing on her bed. She was asleep before her head had even hit the pillow.

When Millie woke the following day, there was still no message or missed calls from Sam. She decided that she would go over and check up on him after she had finished having lunch with his mother. Millie arrived early, she always arrived early and easily found somewhere to park. She wasn't really sure what the protocol here was, should she remain outside and wait for Kathy, or should she head inside and save them a table? Millie needn't have worried, a toot had her snapping her head upwards, Kathy waving from the open window of a car as she drove past and pulled into the parking lot. Millie waited until Kathy had caught up with her, the two women embracing with a hug, before linking arms and walking into The Daily Grind Cafe together. They paused just inside the doorway, looking around. Spotting a vacant table off to one side near the large bay window, Milly and Cassie headed in that direction.

"I'm glad you saw this table Millie, it is so busy in here!"

"It always is at lunchtime, it is the best place to come in town, and now with it officially being tourist season, well, chaos," Millie commented.

"Good afternoon ladies." One of the waitstaff greeted them at their table. "Will it just be the two of you today?"

"Yes, thank you."

"Let's get you started with some water." The young teen placed a jug of icy cold water and two glasses on the table between Millie and Kathy. "Here are your menus, I will be back shortly to see if you are ready to order." She handed Kathy and Millie a menu each and then left to go and help at another table.

"I guess you would come here a lot Millie, seeing as how your best friend works here."

"Yes, I'm here most days, Rachel is more like family to me rather than a friend."

"What would you recommend? I usually only stop in for coffee, and occasionally, a slice of their famous chocolate fudge cake."

"Well, I might be a little bit biased, but everything they sell here is good." Millie closed the menu and laid it on the table. "Personally, I intend to order the basket of cheese bread as a starter, a burger with a lot with fries on the side for my main, and although it is not on the menu, I'm going to have the chocolate mousse for dessert."

"Ooh, that sounds delicious! What is on the burger with the lot?"

"Well, you can pretty much add or delete items as you like, but the standard burger with the lot contains a beef patty, onions, cheese, oven baked bacon, fried egg, beetroot, tomato, pineapple, lettuce, and tomato sauce."

"Are you ready to order?"

"Yes, thank you." Millie gave her order, Kathy requesting that she be given the same. "Will you let Rachel know that I am here please?" The wait staff assured Millie that she would and took her order through to the kitchen.

Rachel all but bounced over to Millie and Kathy's table, her apron lightly dusted in a layer of flour and chocolate smudges. Millie made the introductions; Rachel's eyebrows rose ever so slightly but she held her tongue. Her eyes told Millie that she would be discussing this with her later, something that Millie had counted on. Kathy greeted Rachel enthusiastically, pulling her into a hug just as she had with Millie. Although invited, Rachel could not join them for lunch, but she did promise to join them for dessert.

"She seems absolutely delightful." Kathy mused as Rachel walked away.

"She is, she is also one of the most genuine people that I know."

"Will she be your bridesmaid?" The question surprised Millie, although on some level she knew that it should not have. Millie mentally kicked herself, she should have expected this question, it was a perfectly natural question for a future mother-in-law to ask her future daughter in law, wasn't it? Merely debated for a moment, and then decided to answer any questions related to her engagement as if it was a real engagement.

"Yes, Rachel will be my bridesmaid. In fact, she will be my only attendant, I could not imagine walking down the aisle without her by my side, and just as importantly, there is no one else who I would want to be there supporting me on that day." This at least was the truth.

"Have you and Sam talked about a date yet?"

"No, I think we will wait until after Christmas to choose a date. My brother, Joshua, is in the army, but he has leave over Christmas, so will come home to join us."

"Oh, my goodness, I just had a brilliant idea!" Kathy exclaimed, making Millie feel very nervous. "Why don't you get married at Christmas time? It will be perfect, and your brother will already be here. That way you wouldn't have to wait until he got leave granted again."

"Honestly, I hadn't really thought about it. I mean, Sam only proposed a few days ago."

"Of course, I'm sorry, I'm rushing you, aren't I? I don't mean to, really, I don't, it is just that we have waited so long for Sam to finally settle down, and now that he has, I guess his father and I feel like there is no reason to wait to marry, especially as you have known each other most of your life."

"I understand, honestly I do. I guess I just don't want to rush, I want to fully experience every minute little detail. It isn't about the wedding for me, it is the marriage I want, more than the wedding day, and with that in mind, I have never actually even considered what my own wedding day might be like."

"Well, there will be plenty of time to think about that now. I suppose that you will do all of the planning yourself, no outsourcing?"

"No, I intend to plan my own wedding. With your help of course." Millie smiled across the table at Kathy who smiled back at her. Millie had planned enough weddings to realise that the reason Kathy was so concerned about the wedding plans, was because she was feeling left out. Their entrees came, and as they ate, they chatted about their respective families, and about their plans over Christmas. During their main course, Millie and Kathy spoke about generic happenings within the town of Maitland. By the time that Rachel brought their desert over to the table, the conversation between Kathy and Millie had steered back around to wedding talk.

"Personally, I think that Millie would look amazing in a blush pink wedding dress, rather than a common old white one."

"Rachel!" Millie shot her friend a look that could kill. Why was Rachel helping to perpetuate this lie? Millie was trying to keep the wedding talk as benign as possible, not give out specific details that would inspire hope and connectedness between Kathy and Millie. It wasn't that Millie didn't like Kathy, she did, in fact, had this been an actual engagement, Millie would have been overjoyed to have Kathy joining her life. It was just that Millie had learnt to protect her heart a long time ago, she knew that the closer you allowed people to get to you, the easier it was for them to betray you, to hurt you. Millie was trying to protect herself, her heart, from the pain she knew would follow if she allowed herself to feel or to act as if this was a real engagement. Millie did not want to get hurt, and she did not want to be the cause of another person's hurt either.

"No, that's quite alright Millie dear, we don't need to talk about your dress if you would rather not. I remember when I was newly engaged, trying to find my own voice, scared to speak out against my future mother-in-law and her plans for my wedding." Kathy sighed.

"Well, that was a long time ago, but I often wonder if our relationship would not have been quite so strained if only I had stood my ground from the beginning."

Millie didn't know quite what to say, and Kathy didn't seem to be expecting an answer. Rachel poured them all more coffee, and the three ladies sat and talked well into the afternoon, sharing bits and pieces of themselves, of their lives. As Millie farewelled Kathy out the front of the Daily Grind Cafe, she kissed the older woman softly on the cheek, promising her that she and Sam would be over later in the week for dinner. Millie waved once more to Kathy as they passed each other in the road, Kathy headed west, and Millie headed east. She needed to see Sam, to find out why he had blown her off, to find out what his excuse was for not answering her calls, and for not returning them either. Considering how determined Sam had been to get Millie to agree to be his fake fiancé in the first place, it didn't really seem like he would just ignore her, ghost her, and yet Millie wasn't sure what else it could be. She sighed as she pulled into Sam's driveway, there was mail in the letterbox, was he out of town? Why on earth would he leave without telling her? She stopped her car momentarily and jumped out, opening his mailbox and fishing out all of the contents. Returning to her car, she threw his stack of letters and catalogues on her front passenger seat and continued up the driveway.

Parking her car in the carport, Millie gathered up the mail that she had dropped onto the passenger seat, stuffed it all in her bag, and got out of the car. Crossing to the house she noticed that Sam's car was parked in the garage, and the house looked empty. Millie knew that Sam would never take a taxi anywhere, preferring to drive himself, so where was he? She knocked loudly on the front door, waiting. When there was no answer, she walked across to the guesthouse and knocked on the front door there. After a couple of minutes, and no answer to her knocking, Millie walked back to the main house, using her fist to pound on the front door. Exasperated, Millie walked around to the back of the house and started to knock on the back door. Cupping her hands against the glass of the window, Millie peered into the back of the house but saw no sign of Sam. Irritated, and annoyed at the lack of response from Sam over the past couple of days, Millie knocked again, louder this time, calling out to Sam, letting him know that she was there, to no avail. Millie tried the door handle, jumping in surprise to find it wasn't locked, and that it easily swung open. Millie entered Sam's house, walking through the mudroom and the laundry, to the kitchen. She dropped Sam's mail on the kitchen bench and started walking through the house, room by room, looking for Sam. Not finding him anywhere downstairs, Millie went up to the first floor, again going from room to room, by now convinced that she would surely find his murdered and mangled body somewhere.

Swinging open the last door left on this floor, Millie came face to face with a very wet, very toned, very naked Sam.

CHAPTER NINE

"Oh, my word." Millie's eyes involuntarily travelled down the entire length of Sam's naked body, and painstakingly slowly back up again. Stop, she wanted to scream to herself, stop looking at him, but her traitorous eyes would not listen. He was glorious. Millie could feel the blush creeping up her neck, felt the way her jaw slackened, and fervently wished that the floor would open up and swallow her whole.

"Hello Millie," Sam's voice sounded like a whisper, the blood rushing in Millie's ears making a deafening sound. "So...Do you see anything that you like?"

"I..." Millie's face was on fire, so mortified was she, she was sure that at any moment now she would spontaneously combust. Or rather, she sure hoped that she would.

"You're speechless Millie, really? Now that is interesting." Millie tried in vain to speak, but no words came out. "As much as I would love to stand here all day, I'm naked, which I believe you have already noticed, so if you don't mind,

I would like to get some clothes on before I freeze to death." Millie nodded dumbly, turning on her heel and walking back downstairs to the kitchen, where she fixed herself a strong coffee.

Sam joined her in the kitchen shortly, Millie furiously avoided his gaze.

"Have you been away?" Millie managed to squeak out.

"Nope." Sam brushed past her on his way to the coffee maker, pouring himself a large mug of the black nectar.

"Are you avoiding me?" Millie accused.

"Is that why you came here, to confront me?"

"Confront you? This isn't some B grade detective movie Sam, believe it or not, I was actually worried about you. Why didn't you return any of my calls?"

"Sorry Millie, I didn't know you had called. My phone is around here somewhere..." Millie watched as Sam absently started shuffling items around on the kitchen counter, presumably looking for his lost phone. Millie rolled her eyes and started helping him to look.

"Where did you have it last?"
"Hmm?"

"Your phone Sam, where did you have it last?"

"Oh, I'm not sure, it must be here somewhere," Sam mumbled, wandering off. When he didn't immediately reappear, Millie went after him.

"Sam." Millie quirked an eyebrow, surprised to see him flopped on the sofa in the lounge room. "Are you alright?"

"Huh? Oh, hi Millie."

"Oh, for Pete's sake Sam! Are you drunk?"

"No, my head is just really fuzzy." Millie leant over Sam and pressed the back of her hand to his forehead.

"Sam! You're burning up! How long have you been sick like this?"

"Since yesterday, don't worry, I'm sure I'll be fine, I just need to rest."

"You need more than just rest, Sam, when was the last time you had anything to eat? Drink?"

"My coffee..." Sam pointed to his mug on the coffee table.

"Is not what you need Sam, honestly." Millie shook her head. "I'm calling your mum; you need someone who can come and make sure you don't keel over." She pulled her phone out of her pocket, but before she could dial the number her wrist was grabbed in a vice-like grip. "Sam!" She dropped her phone to the floor.

"Millie, please, don't call mum, I'll be fine." Millie looked down at Sam, contemplating his request. "She would only worry Millie, you know that, besides, she can be a bit...Overwhelming when she has to look after anyone who is sick." He finished lamely.

"Sam, are you scared of your mum?" Millie filed the information away for future use.

"Not scared exactly, just..." He paused, shooting her a smirk. "You know Millie if you are that concerned about my health, you could always stay here and look after me yourself."

"Ha ha, very funny Sam."

"No, I mean it. Why shouldn't you? After all, we are engaged. Imagine how it would look Millie if you have to call my mum and ask her to come and look after me when you are just sitting here all along. I don't know about you, but I would find that highly suspicious." She narrowed her eyes at him, knowing that he was right, he would look suspicious.

"Just what exactly would this looking after you look like Sam? Bed baths and foot massages?"

"In my dreams," Sam muttered, barely loud enough for Millie to hear him. "Fine, don't stay Millie, but can you just do one thing for me before you go, please?"

"Possibly. What is it?"

"I am kind of hungry actually," he looked embarrassed to admit it, "there should be a can of soup in the cupboard, would you warm it up for me please?"

"Canned soup? Seriously?" Millie rolled her eyes. "Fine. I'll stay, just for tonight, and I'll be sleeping in one of the spare bedrooms."

Millie rummaged around in Sam's refrigerator until she found the ingredients that she needed, chopping, peeling and slicing, adding everything into the electric frying pan, and leaving it to simmer. She wandered upstairs, opening the door to the first of many spare bedrooms, and throwing her bag on the bed. Back downstairs the timer was buzzing, Sam's stew was ready. Millie ladled it into a bowl, placing the bowl, and some thick buttered bread, onto a plate, carrying it out to Sam.

"Here, eat this, you'll feel better."

"Thank you." Sam took the plate and started eating, Millie not at all surprised to see how quickly it was disappearing.

"Why do you have such a large house when it is just you that lives here?"

"It seemed like a good idea at the time, besides, it won't be me that lives alone here forever. One day, a wife maybe, a couple of kids. If nothing else, it is a good investment."

"How is your stew?"

"It's really great Millie, thank you. What is it?"

"It's my grandfather's recipe, he used to call it garbage stew. Basically, it is every single thing that you have in the fridge, that is either almost ready to be thrown out or something that you have only used half of. Hence the name garbage." Sam nodded, a long yawn escaping. "Alright Sam, come on, back to bed with you." Millie helped Sam as he stumbled to his feet, dragging his arm across her shoulders, and snaking her arm around his waist, she guided him towards the stairs. It took Millie longer than she thought it would, helping Sam up the stairs, down the hallway, and back through to his bedroom. Millie couldn't help but have a look around once she was inside, the room was luxuriously proportioned, all of the soft furnishings opulent and plush. If this was Millie's bedroom, she would most likely never leave.

She helped Sam over to his king-sized bed, pushing him gently down onto the mattress and covering him with the blanket folded at the foot of the bed.

"Just lay down and rest Sam, I will go to see if I can find you some painkillers." Millie tried the door opposite the bed, discovering a walk-in wardrobe instead of a bathroom. The second door that she tried was more successful, revealing a large bathroom. Millie crossed to the sink, opening the cupboard above it and taking stock. She found the painkillers she was hoping for, along with a glass that she filled with water, taking them all back to Sam and offering them to him. He swallowed the pills easily, and Millie took the glass downstairs to be washed before returning it to the bathroom. By the time Millie returned with the clean glass, Sam was already fast asleep, snoring softly. Millie was struck by just how vulnerable, and how uber sexy he looked, while he was asleep.

"Stop it," she scolded herself softly. "You are not interested, remember? Is only for two weeks, just stay focused girl."

The rest of the afternoon passed peacefully for Millie, she potted around downstairs, tidying up as best she could. The place was a mess, Millie wondered just how long Sam had been feeling sick. She knew that he only had a cold, but still, she could not shake the niggling thought of what might have happened had he been seriously ill. It was something that Millie worried about herself, and perhaps the most annoying thing about being single, about living alone. With the kitchen back to order, Millie set about getting dinner started, wrapping a couple of large potatoes in foil, and placing them in the oven to bake. When she had been hunting out ingredients for her garbage soup earlier on, she had spotted some bacon rashers, which she now diced and placed in a frying pan on the stovetop, ready for frying once the potatoes were baked and ready. While she waited for the potatoes, Millie did a load of washing, pegging it out to dry. Millie ran a mop over the kitchen and dining room floors and peeked in on Sam, who was still sound asleep, before sitting down at the kitchen table and pulling out her phone. Millie sat for a few minutes, using her phone to check her emails, answering those that were most important, and filing those that she could deal with later.

Millie set the table and went to wake Sam. He joined her in the kitchen as she was starting to plate up, taking a seat at the table and watching her through hooded eyes.

"This looks great Millie, thank you."

"You're welcome, it is nothing fancy, but they are delicious, and they are filling."

"You sell yourself short, Millie. Baked potato topped with grated cheese and diced bacon has always been one of my favourite meals."

"That's because potato and bacon are comfort foods." Millie smiled across at him.

"It is true what they say," Sam smiled back, "the way to a man's heart is through his stomach." He winked at Millie.

"Well, lucky for me, I already own your heart." Millie flashed her engagement ring at him.

"Indeed, you do." A chill shot down Millie's back, at the sincerity of the words.

The rest of the evening passed in quiet company, Sam watched some television while

Millie flicked through a Christmas catalogue that Sam had on the coffee table.

"I adore Christmas." Millie mused aloud. "Have you finished all of your gift shopping?"

"The perks of having a small family." Sam muted the television to look at Millie. "I tend to get the same thing each year anyway, my brother has pretty specific tastes, which makes him easy to shop for. As for my parents, my brother and I tend to go halves on something extravagant for them. Last year we sent them to the Maldives for a fortnight, this year we arranged for their portrait to be painted by an artist from Sydney, his work has hung in the National Portrait Gallery and is one of mum and dad's favourite artists."

"That's nice."

"What about you? Shopped for Josh yet."

"Yup, new techy stuff." At Sam's raised eyebrow, Millie elaborated. "He gave me a list, I just showed it to the store clerk, and voila! His gift was purchased."

"I'm sure he'll love it."

"I hope so. Hey, what's this?" Millie held up a thick cream coloured envelope, closed with a rich gold ribbon.

"Our invitations for tomorrow night's Christmas party at work."

"Tomorrow night?!"

"Yes, did you forget? I am sure that we talked about it."

"Yes, we did, I just completely forgot that it was tomorrow night." Millie fretted. "What on earth will I wear? Is it black tie? Or more casual?"

"It is definitely black tie Millie, it is being hosted at the Star hotel in Sydney."

"The Star? I've never been there, but I have heard about it, it is supposed to be one of the most exclusive hotels in the world, perfect for the discerning guest, they originated in the middle east and now have over twenty locations throughout the world."

"You have done your research." Sam sounded impressed.

"One of my recent brides was hoping to stay there, but it was out of budget."

"The Christmas party will start at eight o'clock in the evening, I thought that we would leave here at midday, that will give us plenty of time to drive down there, to check in to the hotel, and to get ready for the evening."

"That sounds nice. Hang on, did you say that we would be checking in to the hotel? As in, staying there overnight?"

"Yes. The party most likely won't wrap up until the early hours of the morning, and it will be far too late to drive back then. Is that a problem?"

"No, not at all. Um, Sam, you did book us into two rooms, right?"

"One room, two double beds. I can't have my staff wondering why my own fiancé requires a separate hotel room now, can I?"

"No, I guess not."

"What are you going to be wearing?"

"A tuxedo, why?"

"Black?"

"Yes."

"I'm just planning on what to wear."

"Anything you choose will be fine Millie, you look sexy in everything."

"Thank you, I hadn't realised that you took that much notice."

"I'm still a man Millie, and believe me, everyone notices you." Millie flushed under his gaze. "I need to go to bed, my head is throbbing. We'll swing past your house first thing tomorrow, so you can grab something to wear."

"Okay." Millie's eyes watched him as he made his way across the room to the staircase.

"And   Millie?"
"Yes."
"Thank you."
"For what?"
"For being here and playing nursemaid, I do appreciate it."
"You're welcome. Go on, off to bed, I will bring up some water and more painkillers just as soon as I do the dishes." Millie left a glass of water and the box of painkillers on Sam's bedside table, in case he woke in the night and needed them. It felt weird to Millie, snuggling down in bed in Sam's spare bedroom, with him sleeping only a few feet away. Pushing her thoughts aside, Millie went over the plan for tomorrow, excitement building, the promise of adventure bringing a smile to her face. Mentally picturing her wardrobe, Millie was sound asleep before she could even decide on what she was going to wear.

CHAPTER TEN

"Millie, you look absolutely beautiful!" Sam was looking at her intently, his gaze lingering. Millie had just stepped out of the dressing room in their hotel room, dressed in a Christmas green floor-length stretch lace evening gown, featuring scattered rhinestone detailing and an open keyhole back that hugged her curves in all the right places.

"Thank you, you look gorgeous yourself." Millie took a moment to look Sam up and down. Having had a great night sleep last night, he had woken up this morning feeling much better, and ready to party. One thing was for sure, Sam certainly knew how to rock a tuxedo! Millie did a slow turn in front of Sam, not missing the way his eyes darkened. She knew that she looked good but having him confirm it was that much sweeter.

"May I?" Sam offered Millie his arm.

"Thank you." Millie took his arm, smiling up at him, ignoring the zing of excitement that ran up her arm. This was business, nothing else, she reminded herself sternly.

They walked slowly down the hallway, Millie soaking up all of the rich décor, trying not to be too obvious in the way that she looked from side to side, wanting to remember every small detail, not wanting to miss anything.

"I'll make sure to take some photos for you before we leave." Sam joked as she gawped at yet another gold gilded mirror.

"Very funny." Millie swatted him on the chest. "Unlike some people, I won't get a chance to come back here anytime soon, I want to make sure that I don't miss anything!"

"You don't know that. If all goes well tonight, my company will be back here next year, if you are free, maybe you will agree to accompany me as my plus one."

"Maybe," Millie murmured, not ready to commit to spending any more time in a fantasy world with Sam.

As they stepped into the lift, Sam pulled her close to his side, wrapping his arm around her waist, and dropping his head to whisper in her ear.

"In case I forget to tell you this later Millie, it is an honour to have you on my arm tonight, thank you." Speechless, Millie cupped Sam's cheek in her hand, placing a soft, chaste, kiss on his lips, much the way a friend would.

"You're welcome."

Millie could not stop the gasp from escaping as she laid eyes on the ballroom for the first time. To suggest that it was exquisite would be an understatement. Millie had known that it was going to be a big space, Sam had told her that it was over seven thousand six hundred square feet, yet even she had not imagined a space of this magnitude. The room was crowned by a dramatic cathedral style ceiling, beautifully lit with crystal chandeliers. Floor to ceiling windows ran the entire length of the ballroom, draped with luxurious fabric. The walls were painted in a creamy colour palette, ensuring that the Christmas colour scheme and décor that was chosen by Sam's company really popped. For Millie though, the real piece de resistance was the fact that the ballroom opened out of one end, to reveal an intimate yet well-proportioned courtyard, resplendent with bench seats and cosy little alcoves, perfect for partaking in a secret rendezvous. Not that

Millie was planning on having a secret rendezvous, certainly not with anybody here tonight. Her eyes involuntarily slid over to Sam. As much as she might be tempted, and boy was she tempted, especially seeing him like this, in all his billionaire glory, luxury oozing from his paws, power emanating off him in waves, she knew better than to get involved with a man like Sam.

A waiter dressed in white tie offered them a tray of champagne, the crystal flutes sparkling under the chandeliers. Sam took two, passing one to her.
"A toast. To us." He smiled as she clinked her glass softly against his.
"To us." Millie echoed, tasting the sweetness of the champagne, the bubbles exploding on her tongue. It was sheer delight. Millie had not tasted anything like it before, the weddings that she planned usually opted for wine and spirits over champagne. A shame really.
"When we marry Sam, I want this champagne served at our wedding."
"Millie, are you feeling alright?" Sam looked at her, confusion on his face.
"I'm fine," she shrugged.

"It's just that you have never spoken about our engagement with such familiarity, such normalcy before, it almost sounds real." Millie didn't say anything, the truth was, she had gotten carried away, a fact that she did not want Sam to know. "So, champagne it is." "Thank you, I decided long ago that my wedding would have champagne, I want the fairy tale." Millie smiled.

"Come on," Sam tugged at her hand gently, "I want to introduce you to my core team, mostly executives and their wives, and maybe one or two designers." Sam led her across the ballroom, they were not the last to arrive, but Millie had been surprised to see just how many people were already there, ready to party. By the looks of a few of the guests, they had started the party early, hours earlier. She wondered if they would last the distance, or if they would be quietly asked to leave.

"I hired out the entire hotel, all the staff have rooms here for the night." Sam broke into her thoughts as if reading her mind.

"Millie, I would like you to meet my vice president of operations, Martin King, and his wife, Sandy. Martin, Sandy, may I present my fiancé, Millie."

"Fiancé! Sam, this is fantastic news, congratulations!" Martin pumped Sam's hand up and down vigorously.

"Millie, I'm so happy to finally meet you, Sam talks about you a lot," Sandy spoke softly, Millie liked her instantly, she could see why Sam had made Martin his vice president of operations, he was obviously a huge cheerleader and supporter of Sam, it was natural, there was clearly a deep friendship there.

Sam and Millie stood there speaking with Martin and Sandy for a few more minutes, before reluctantly excusing themselves to mingle some more.

"They seem lovely."

"They are." Sam agreed.

"What did you tell Sandy about me?" Millie couldn't help being curious, Sam had been talking about her.

"It isn't important."

"Sam." Millie stopped in her tracks, looking at him expectantly.

"Millie," Sam sighed, "it isn't important, I promise you, but seeing as how you seem determined to find out, I will tell you later, this is not the place."

"Later then." Millie smiled at him, determined to keep him to his word. Millie acted her part to perfection, she was the ideal fiancé, smiling at the wives, remembering names, laughing at the cheesy jokes the employees told in their nervousness. She showed her ring off to anyone who asked, not missing the pride in Sam's voice as he introduced her as his fiancé time and time again. Eventually, they made their way through the entire ballroom, ending up not far from where they had started, a relieved Millie excusing herself to use the ladies' room.

Millie could have stayed in the ladies' room for hours, so well-appointed it was. A sitting room with plush sofas and coffee tables was arranged around a large television, there was a small kitchenette, and private booths for making telephone calls. There were also ten private bathrooms, shamefully larger than her own bathroom at home. As Millie was reapplying her lipstick in the mirror, the blonde that Sam had introduced as Amanda sidled up to her, the fakest grin that Millie had ever seen plastered on her face.

"Where has Sam been hiding you away?"

"Excuse me?"

"Well, we've never heard of you until today, and yet here you are, engagement ring and all." The venom in Amanda's voice was thick with jealousy, causing more than a few heads to turn in their direction. Millie wondered if Amanda was the only one who had harboured an unrequited crush on Sam and if she was the real reason that he had asked for Millie's help.

"Well, that's at my request." Millie gave Amanda her sweetest smile. "Our private life is just that, private. With both of us running successful businesses, often featured in the social pages of the newspapers, we keep our family life to ourselves, and our closest friends of course."

"Of course." It really was true, if looks could kill, Millie would be a dead woman right now. "So, when's the big day?" Amanda tried a different tactic.

"Sorry Amanda, but that is personal. As I am sure you will understand, Sam and I are not inviting his employees to our wedding or reception. If you are asking when you need to start calling me Millie Marsden, you can do that once Sam returns from Christmas leave." Millie smiled at Amanda, capped her lipstick and returned it to her bag. "Now, if you will excuse me, my fiancé is waiting to dance with me again." With a nod at Amanda, Millie turned away from the mirror and left the room, keen to find Sam and to fill him in on what she suspected that he already knew in regard to Amanda.

Sam was waiting just where she had left him, she smiled in spite of herself. She had told him that she would be fine, that he didn't need to wait for her, that she would come and find him if she needed to, and yet he had waited. He knew that she didn't like crowds, had known this since they first met years ago. He also knew why, with her mother always in the spotlight, Millie had craved normalcy as a child, had yearned to have a private life with no one gawking at her on the street. Had only gotten that once her mother and stepfather had died, leaving her and her brother in the care of their grandfather. It was a high price to pay for the privacy that she craved, and one that as a child, she had blamed herself for, convinced that some higher power had heard her wish for a simple life, and had misconstrued it. With the help of her grandfather, and a child psychologist, Millie had come to realise that it was not her fault, that the car crash that had killed her mother and stepfather had simply been an accident.

"Dance with me?" Sam greeted her once she reached his side. Millie nodded, allowing Sam to take her hand and lead her out onto the dancefloor.

"I met Amanda," Millie whispered in Sam's ear as he pulled her close against his chest. Was that a groan she heard from him?

"Ignore her." His hand down her back to rest just above the roundness of her bottom.

"She has a crush on you." Suddenly flushed, Millie wished that they were dancing closer to the window.

"Unreciprocated, I assure you." Sam's voice was low, intimate.

"I know." Millie gasped as Sam unexpectedly dipped her.

"Millie," Sam looked at her intently, his tone serious, "no matter what people gossip about, I give you my word, as long as I am with you, I will be faithful. As if I could ever want anyone else when all I need is right here in my arms."

Millie knew that Sam was going to kiss her even before his head started to dip towards hers. She knew it and yet she didn't move away.

His lips were gentle, familiar somehow. His tongue prodded her mouth open, she willingly complied. Their tongues danced, gently at first, before fighting for dominance. Sam tilted her head back, angling her face to deepen their kiss. Her skin was on fire. Her hands tangled in his hair, she could feel the weight of his erection against her stomach. Suddenly Sam broke the kiss, wrenching away from Millie, both of them gasping for breath, Millie's chest heaving.

"Let's get out of here." Gripping her hand in a vice like hold, Sam strode out of the ballroom, Millie at his side, headed for the lifts. They stood in silence, waiting for the lift to arrive, the muscle in Sam's jaw working overtime. Once inside the lift, Sam swiped his card for the penthouse suite, pushing the door close button, ensuring their privacy.

He turned to Millie, a predatory grin slowly forming on his face, as he advanced towards her slowly. He captured her mouth in his, pinning her against the lift wall, an arm on either side of her trembling body. His arm snaked down, dancing across Millie's side, down further, across the swell of her bottom, down her thigh, to lift her leg up, pressing his erection closer to her core. Millie gasped in delight, wrapping her arms around his back, urging him closer to her. Sam trailed a line of kisses down Millie's jawline, and over her neck, cupping her breast through the fabric of her dress. Millie moaned and thrust her chest out, desperate to have him closer still.

"Millie, do you have any idea what you do to me?" Sam ground out, before claiming her mouth, his fierce hunger evident in the way his mouth ground into hers, unrelenting.

"Sam, I-". Millie was stopped from answering by the ding of the elevator doors opening. They had reached the penthouse.

Under the glaring lights of the penthouse, Millie's sanity returned. She knew she must look a sight, her lips were swollen from Sam's kisses, a delightful tenderness, and her dress felt rumpled. Looking at Sam, he hadn't fared much better. His shirt was almost completely unbuttoned, Millie blushed to realise that she must have been responsible for that in the elevator, and his hair was completely out of order. Millie knew that she could not allow herself to sleep with Sam, and yet still...If he asked her, she knew that she wouldn't refuse. Her body all but sang for his touch.

"Millie, forgive me, that was inappropriate."

"Sam," Millie smiled at him, crossing to stand closer, reaching up to try and straighten up his hair, "don't ever apologise for kissing me. We both know that we are equally to blame." She stepped back. "In another life Sam, I would jump into bed with you right now."

"But not tonight," Sam stated.

"No." Millie shook her head ruefully, wondering if she would regret her decision.

"Goodnight Millie." Sam smiled, Millie was grateful that he didn't contradict her or argue with her.

"Goodnight Sam." She kissed him on the cheek, turning to walk slowly through to the bedroom, Sam having previously agreed to take the plush sofa for the night. It was a long and restless night, neither Millie nor Sam managing to get any sleep at all, both too wound up with thoughts of the person on the other side of the wall to relax enough for sleep to claim them.

CHAPTER ELEVEN

The car ride home had been sweet torture for Millie, her traitorous hands were itching to just reach over and hold Sam's hand, or to rest on his thigh. She giggled as she imagined what his reaction to either might be. In the end, they had made it home in one piece, Sam walking her to the door and telling her to get some sleep before he picked her up later that evening. Although they were attending Belinda and Greg's wedding rehearsal dinner as a couple, Millie was still going to be working, and she would need to look the part, something which only came after several hours of sleep.

A long hot shower and a nice cup of tea helped Millie to relax to the point where she was able to finally fall asleep. Her sleep was dreamless, and she woke, refreshed, shortly before two o'clock in the afternoon. There wasn't much that Millie had to do for the rehearsal dinner, it pretty much took care of itself. Belinda and Greg had decided after much discussion that they wanted to be married at Barb and Ron's house, Belinda wanted to marry at her childhood home, she wanted the feeling of closing that chapter as she started her married life, and her first time living away from home. It was symbolic for her and very emotional for Barb and Ron. While the wedding would be an outdoor affair, Belinda and Greg had decided to hold their rehearsal dinner inside, meaning that all unnecessary furniture had to be moved into the storage shed for the evening, replaced with white wooden chairs and the boho decor that Belinda had so fallen in love with.

Sam picked Millie up promptly at four o'clock in the afternoon, hands stuffed firmly in his suit pockets, a wry smile on his face as he kept his distance. Millie's eyes roamed across Sam's face, drinking him all in, feasting on the way he looked in his custom-made suit. There was a dull ache inside Millie, one she was content to ignore, not wanting to name it as if by denying it a name she could deny its existence. The car ride over to Barb and Ron's house was quiet, too quiet as far as Millie was concerned. She missed Sam, which she knew sounded crazy, he was right next to her, physically at least, although she suspected mentally and emotionally, he was light years away from her. She knew that she should never have kissed him, was angry with herself for doing so, she had made this situation far more complicated than it had ever needed to be, and she had no one to blame but herself. It was a relief to finally pull into Barb and Ron's driveway, it gave Millie the excuse that she needed to leave Sam's presence, she had to go and find Barb and Belinda and make sure that everything was okay and that there were no last minute problems that she needed to sort out.

When Millie finally located Barb, she was happy to discover that the majority of the work had been carried out, Millie's team of workers having arrived hours earlier. The furniture had been stored, and the new decor all set up. The change was immaculate, the house no longer felt like a home, but rather like an opulent space for weddings. Millie checked that the caterers had everything in hand, unlike Belinda's kitchen tea, her rehearsal dinner was to be a sit-down affair, with six scrumptious courses for her guests to feast on, and Millie wanted everything to be perfect. Millie fussed around with the flowers and the party bags, arranging everything just so, waiting for Belinda to finish getting ready. She was not, Millie assured herself, trying to avoid Sam, not at all.

Belinda came downstairs shortly before half-past five in the evening, looking every bit as radiant as a bride to be should look. The guests started arriving shortly after, and by six o'clock in the evening, the minister was all set up and ready to get started. Millie ushered all of the guests to their seats, nodding for the violinist to begin. She slid into her seat next to Sam just as Belinda entered the room on her father's arm. Although only a rehearsal, it was a wonderful ceremony, and Millie knew that the real thing was going to be one heck of an emotional day, for both Belinda and her mother, the two were as close as Millie had ever seen a mother and daughter.

The following dinner was a noisy happy affair. Millie found herself seated between Sam and his mother Kathy, who was delighted to have the opportunity to spend time with Millie. Millie found it especially hard to concentrate on what Kathy was saying, sitting so close to Sam, she found herself flushed and tongue tied.

Millie wondered if Sam knew the effect he was having on her, when his fingers accidentally brushed against her hand, lingering for a fraction longer than necessary, Millie suspected that he did in fact know. Deciding that two could play this game, Millie leant closer to Sam, cupping his cheek with one hand, turning her body slightly to hide her other hand from view, looking for all intents and purposes as a loved-up fiancé whispering in her lover's ear.

"I know what you are doing Sam," Millie whispered quietly, slipping her hand under the table and across his thigh, her nails lightly scraping across the thin fabric covering his bulge, feeling him jerk beneath her.

Before she could move her hand, he captured it, holding it in place, watching her face intently as he grew large beneath her hand. Millie's lips parted slightly, it was a heady feeling, knowing that she was responsible for Sam's erection, the knowledge emboldened her and without another thought, she leant over and kissed him solidly on the mouth, the aching peaks of her nipples pressing into his chest. The polite cough of the waiter serving dessert had Millie drawing away from Sam, her attention now completely focused on her dessert, a chocolate concoction topped with fresh strawberries. She studied the dessert as if her life depended upon it, refusing to look at Sam for the remainder of the evening.

Once the last piece of furniture had been placed back in its original position, and the last guest had been thanked and farewelled, Millie bid Barb, Belinda, Greg and Ron goodnight, taking Sam's hand and allowing him to lead her out to his car. He waited until she was settled before closing her door, such a small act, one that Millie found incredibly comforting. He was thoughtful like that, always putting her needs first. She wondered if that would extend to the bedroom as well? Maybe, if she was brave enough, once this whole wedding was finished, she would find out. It was an interesting thought. He dropped her home like a gentleman. The following day would be a big one for Millie, she was preparing the house for Belinda's wedding, she would marry Greg the day after, and then it would be a matter of days until Millie and Sam would end their agreement. Millie wondered how she would feel once it was all over, somehow she already knew that she was going to miss Sam.

CHAPTER TWELVE

Millie looked around and smiled. The space was stunning, every surface sparkled with hundreds of tiny fairy lights, Belinda's bloom of choice, gardenias, lined the makeshift aisle that led from the house across the lawn to the gazebo where Greg was currently waiting for his bride. With all the guests seated, the minister at his pulpit, Millie nodded to Barb, it was time. Barb wiped a stray tear from her eye and then nodded, stepping out into the garden, and beginning her slow walk down the aisle, smiling and nodding at the guests as she went. Once Barb was seated the violinist stood up, lifted her bow, and started to play. As the first few notes of the bridal march were played, the guests rose, turning to catch a look at Belinda as she came down the aisle on her proud father's arm. Belinda was radiant, the dress she chose custom made for her by an internationally famous designer, and friend of her mother's. What made her shine was not the dress, however, but rather the love that sparkled in her eyes, there was no doubt to those in attendance that this was a marriage of love, and one that would last, Millie hoped, for all of time. As Millie sat and watched the ceremony take place, Sam by her side, his fingers looped through hers, she couldn't help but imagine her own wedding day.

She knew that if she ever married, it would not be a big deal, she certainly did not want five hundred guests like Belinda had, no, Millie would prefer something intimate, her closest friends only, maybe a dozen guests. She smiled at the thought, imagine Sam or his mother agreeing to that. No, they would expect a society wedding. Sam squeezed her hand, she looked up at him, saw his raised eyebrow, questioning her. She smiled and winked, feeling him relax. She leaned against his shoulder and sighed. Sometimes, she could very well imagine herself marrying a man like Sam, even liked the idea. It would be nice, occasionally, to have someone look after her, but nice always ended. Of the two boyfriends that Millie had acquired over the years, one had drifted off once they found out that they preferred men, and the other one had cheated on her with a university friend. Millie had been less hurt than she knew she should have been and had later planned their wedding, no hard feelings between any of them. She didn't think that the same would be said should Sam heat on her, despite them only pretending to be engaged.

Vows over, the kiss, and, at Millie's prior arrangement, perfectly timed fireworks. A cheer went up from the crowd, the surprise fireworks a great hit. The waiters started mingling, wine glasses on their trays. As the bride and groom stole away for photographs, the hired orchestra began playing, entertaining the guests with a variety of music. Millie went through to the kitchen, making sure that the wait staff had remembered to pack two trays of horsd'oeuvres, which she now carried through to the private roped off garden where the photographer was hard at work, along with a bottle of wine and several wine glasses. In her experience, the bridal party looked happier in the photographs if they were well fed beforehand.

With the photographs finished, the happy couple was welcomed into the reception by a round of applause, as they made their way around the tables, greeting their dear friends, sharing in everyone's joy at their union. Dinner was a sumptuous feast, eight courses consisting of locally grown and sourced ingredients, all contributing towards dishes such as marinated lamb shanks in a red wine jus; fresh lobster with homemade mango chutney; the cutest baked baby potatoes; crusty bread rolls; and locally grown and pressed coffee. Belinda's wedding cake, a massive twelve tiers, had alternate layers of apricot cake and chocolate mud cake and had been decorated in nine thousand hand created apricot coloured bud roses. Stunning was an understatement. Belinda and Greg had opted to have the cake boxed as part of their wedding favours, the guests instead helping themselves to an array of desserts from the dessert bar provided.

The entire night was a huge success, as Belinda and Greg took to the dancefloor for their first dance as husband and wife, Millie found herself staring across the dancefloor and into the eyes of Sam, his gaze unwavering, broken only when another guest clapped him on the shoulder, engaging him in conversation. Millie turned away; her emotions raw. The wedding reception lasted well into the early hours of the morning, Belinda and Greg finally bidding farewell, needing to get to the international airport to board their plane, Belinda having confided to Millie that Greg was taking her to France for their honeymoon. The tears that Barb had held at bay throughout the night came tumbling down when she hugged her daughter goodbye, the two women clinging to each other, until Greg eventually took his new wife in his arms, helping her into their hired limousine. The guests waved until the limousine was out f sight, Millie stood with Barb for a while longer, before helping the older woman back into the house.

The guests didn't linger once Belinda and Greg had left, apart from a few close friends who were staying for the weekend to help Barb and Ron get through the first few days of quiet and loneliness. Once Millie was certain that Barb and Ron would be okay, and once she had supervised for wait staff packing up, Millie gathered up the last remaining items and boxed them, placing them at the back door with the rest of the boxes, she would swing past and pick them up tomorrow afternoon. She gestured to Sam to let him know that she was ready to leave, and together they went and made their goodbyes to Barb and Ron, congratulating them yet again on a wonderful wedding, and an amazing evening. Barb and Ron walked them out to Sam's car, thanking Millie over and over for giving their baby girl the wedding of her dreams, waving them off until their car disappeared into the inky darkness of the early morning. As Millie watched Sam as he drove, every fibre of her being zinging with the success of the evening, she had a sudden plan.

"Sam, stop the car." Sam pulled over in a spray of gravel, cutting the engine.

"What's wrong?" Before she could lose her nerve, Millie reached over and pulled Sam's head down, her lips meeting his in a kiss that left nothing to the imagination. Her hands trailed downwards, tugging at the hem of his shirt, freeing it from his pants, sliding her hands inside to feel his skin beneath hers. "Millie." Sam moaned into her mouth, breaking the kiss and pushing her away slowly.

"You don't want to?" Millie stated matter of fact.

"Millie, hell, of course, I want to!" Sam ran a hand through his hair. "You drive me wild woman, I want nothing more than to take you right now, right here in the front seat of my car, I don't care who might see us, but I can't Millie. If I don't stop now, I won't be able to stop, you understand me."

"Sam, you're sweet." Millie looked him in the eye, not dropping eye contact as she slid her hand under the waistband of his trousers, cupping his erection in her palm. "Take me home Sam, to bed, now." She gave a small squeeze, delighting in the groan that escaped his lips.

"Millie." His lips claimed hers, she undid her seatbelt, sliding across to straddle his lap, her dress riding up to her bottom.

"Millie, Millie, Millie," Sam murmured, trailing kisses down her neck, his hands sliding up her thighs to cup her bottom, exclaiming his delight at finding her skin bare. "You minx you." His fingers kneaded her supple flesh, sliding under her thighs to nudge her legs wider still, her heady scent of arousal filling the car. He slid a finger into her core, slowly, testing her. "Urgh, so wet already, Millie, you're exquisite." He brought his finger up to his mouth, tasting her on his tongue. It was nearly Millie's undoing, watching Sam, and she moved his finger, claiming his mouth with her own instead, lifting herself up off Sam's lap and tugging at his trousers. Taking the hint, Sam tugged his trousers down as far as was possible while sitting in the front seat of a sports car, before he turned his attention to Millie's strapless dress, undoing the zip and tugging it down to her waist, his eyes growing round as her breasts sprang free, her nipples already standing erect.

Holding Millie's hips, he guided her back down onto his lap, his throbbing cock nudging at her bundle of nerves. He ran his hands up to cup Millie's breasts, capturing one in his mouth, sucking on it as if his life depended upon it. He pinched and teased the other one, rolling the sensitive nipple between his thumb and forefinger, as Millie writhed on his lap, arching her back and moaning his name.

"Sam, please, please," Millie begged.

"Tell me what you need honey."

"I need you, now!" Millie couldn't hide the urgency in her voice, her skin was on fire, Sam was the only one who could quell it. Rising to her knees, Millie gripped Sam's erection in her hand, pumping her hand up and down his shaft, watching his eyes darken. Once his breathing started to grow laboured, Millie slowly guided him to her core, lining him up before slowly lowering herself down onto his hardened member, a long, slow moan of bliss escaping her mouth as she did so.

Heaven, that is what this was, heaven. Once she had fully sheathed herself on Sam's thick cock, Millie started to move, slowly at first, and then with more confidence, up and down, moving her hips in circular motions, her breasts swaying and dancing for Sam. Sam's eyes feasted on the sight of her, hypnotised by the way her breasts swayed and danced for him as she met and rode every one of his thrusts, feeling the way her muscles stretched to accommodate his size. Desperate with need and unable to stand the wait any longer, Sam gripped Millie's hips, anchoring her to his shaft as she moved faster and faster. Millie arched her back, taking him deeper still, throwing her head back in a scream of triumph as she orgasmed atop of him, bucking her hips as her release tore through her, screaming his name with wild abandon. Hearing Millie scream his name was Sam's undoing, and it tipped him over the edge, Millie grinding down onto him until his spasms stopped, collapsing onto his chest with a contented sigh of mutual bliss.

Once they had both returned from their lovemaking high, Sam kissed her tenderly, before straightening up her dress and scooting her over into her own seat, buckling her in safely. Tucking his cock, already growing hard again, back into his trousers, Sam started the engine, reaching over to take Millie's hand, holding it in his, resting them both in his lap. It was a long drive home to Sam's house.

CHAPTER THIRTEEN

Millie raced into Sam's house, feeling as free as a teenager, kicking off her shoes and letting her dress fall to the floor at the base of the stairs, standing there, in all of her naked glory, on display for Sam. She should have felt vulnerable, instead, she had never felt safer. She watched, unwavering, while Sam stripped his clothes off, dropping them to join hers on the floor, striding towards her, his magnificent cock jutting out in front of him, erect, rock hard, for her. He was just as sculpted as she knew he would be. She didn't move, happily letting him pin her to the wall, his mouth claiming hers with a fierceness that was primal.

"Do you have any idea how long I have wanted to do this?" Sam ground out. "How long I have wanted you, longed to touch you?" He slid a finger deep into her core, pumping it in and out in quick succession, causing a spasm to shoot through Millie.

"How long?" Millie gasped as he added a second finger inside her silky folds, feeling her pool of wetness wrap around him. Her eyes grew round as he brought his fingers up to his mouth, tasting her, before he moved them back to her core, tweaking her sensitive nub.

Millie writhed against Sam, trying in vain to get closer to him, whimpering with need.
"Since we were teenagers. I had so many wet, filthy dreams about what I would do to you if only you had given me the slightest encouragement." Sam added a third finger to her dripping core, pumping them in and out, twisting them with each deep thrust. Millie bucked her hips against Sam's hand, moving in sync with his fingers thrusting, urging him deeper inside her centre. Sam added his fourth finger to the twisting and pumping, his thumb rubbing across her bundle of nerves. It was Millie's undoing, and she cried out his name, biting down on his shoulder, legs shaking, shudders echoing through her body as she came undone, the most powerful orgasm she had ever had ripping through her body.

"Sam, I-" she smiled up at him shyly.
"Shhh, I love watching you come undone, I love that I can do that to you."

"You're not the only one." Millie dropped to her knees before Sam, licking her lips in anticipation.

"Millie, you don't have to."

"Trust me, Sam, I want to." Eyes never leaving his face, Millie ran her fingers up his inner thighs, taking a testicle into her mouth, sucking gently, rolling it around her tongue, releasing it with a soft nip, before repeating her actions with the other testicle. Still not breaking eye contact, Millie shifted her mouth to Sam's shaft, already coated in a thin layer of his juices. Her tongue darted across the tip of his cock, tasting him, licking her lips. Holding on to his hips, Millie slid her mouth over his hardened length, drawing him deep inside.

Millie's teeth grazed along Sam's length as she slid her mouth up and down his shaft, painstakingly slowly, before building up a rhythm, faster and faster, before slowing back down, determined to draw out his pleasure for as long as she could.

"Millie, I won't last much longer, I'm going to come!" Sam gasped out; his voice thick with need. "I can't...hold on...much longer!" Millie tightened her hold on Sam's hips, taking his thick shaft even deeper into her throat, humming as she did, sending vibrations shooting down his length.

"Millie!" Sam cried out triumphantly and clung to her hair as his orgasm tore through his body. Millie held him steady as he emptied his load into her mouth, licking him clean before kissing his swollen head. Sam pulled Millie into his arms, kissing her deeply. Taking her hand, he led her upstairs, down the hall and into his bedroom, not bothering to close the door.

He cupped her face in his hands, kissing her gently, hearing her contented moan. Sam guided Millie across to the bed, scrambling on after her. Millie smiled up at Sam from between her lashes, as his gaze raked over her body, drinking her in, committing her to memory. Slowly, very slowly, Sam leant down, capturing her mouth in a kiss, his hand sliding down, gliding over Millie's stomach and down further, to cup her centre, growing hard at the discovery of her wetness, idly wondering if the day would ever come when he would tire of knowing that he made her that wet. With a sigh of contentment, he dipped his head to capture her breast, teasing her nipple until he felt it harden and pebble beneath his tongue, suckling and biting, loving the sounds it elicited from Millie. His fingers slipped further down, delving into her silky folds, dipping in and out with a leisurely speed, as Millie moaned and writhed beneath him. Releasing her swollen nipple, Sam moved his attentions lower still, probing his tongue into her very core, teasing, tasting, drinking in her juices, as she bucked her hips beneath him, her breathing growing laboured. Rising to his knees, Sam spread her knees even further apart, wanting to see all of her, loving the sight of having her open for him, knowing that she was his alone. He lent over her, driving his erection into her, before pulling out fully and driving in again.

Millie arched her back and bucked her hips to meet his powerful thrusts, screaming in pleasure as he drove in harder and deeper, his thick member filling her to breaking point, his pelvic bone pressing against her sensitive nub. Millie held nothing back as he moved within her, she was his completely. Pulling his length out fully, he gave one final thrust all the way into her core and felt her walls tighten around his stiffened member as he pushed her over the edge, hearing her scream out his name with wild abandon. With one final thrust he exploded inside her, gripping her hips for support, until totally spent, he collapsed beside her. As they lay nestled in each other's arms, Sam was struck with the thought that being with Millie had felt absolutely perfect, and for the first time in his life, he had forgotten to use any precautions at all tonight.

Hours later, when Millie woke, Sam was still sound asleep, a smile softening his features, his arm splayed across her middle. Millie was filled with regret, not for sleeping with Sam, no, that had been magnificent. Instead, she was full of regret for letting her guard down, for opening her heart and her emotions to Sam and his charms. At some point in the night, she had forgotten that this was a business deal, she had forgotten to guard her heart, and in the process, she had become aware of the very real and unmistakable fact that she was completely and irrevocably in love with Sam Marsden.

CHAPTER FOURTEEN

Panicked, with the realisation that she was in love with Sam hanging over her head, Millie did what any self-respecting coward would do in her situation, she left. Slipping out of bed, her face covered with shame, she wriggled back into her now ruined dress. Spotting a notepad on the kitchen bench, she picked up the accompanying pen and scribbled the following note: Sam, getting a head start on today's massive clean-up job, talk later, M. She left it propped up on the coffee machine, where he was sure to see it first thing, and then slipped quietly out of the back door, using her mobile telephone to call Rachel, who collected her, no questions asked, and dropped her off at home, with the promise of a long conversation later.

Millie stood under the shower, scalding water cascading down her back until she had sufficiently drowned out the voice in her hand, urging her to go back, to explain in person. Millie shut off the water and stepped out of the shower, ruefully eyeing off her crumpled dress laying in a heap on the floor, gathering it up and regretfully throwing it in the bin. Drying off, Millie dressed in a simple pair of jeans and a tank top, pairing them with her most comfortable pair of sneakers. No matter how much she longed to go back to bed, to cry away her shame and her regret, this was a workday for her, and she knew the physical aspect of today would be good for her. With a bit of luck, she would be too tired by the end of the day to do anything more than just crawl into bed and sleep.

When Millie arrived at Barb and Ron's house, it was to find the place deserted. Their housekeeper happily let Millie in, glad of the company, and made them both a hot, strong coffee and a slice of homemade orange cake to enjoy before Millie got started, insisting that she could not possibly lug all of those boxes without something in her stomach to fortify her first. Millie didn't argue, instead sitting, enjoying the cake and the company, before eventually excusing herself to get started. Lugging the boxes out to her car was backbreaking work, by the time Millie was finished, she was covered in a thin layer of dust and grime. She waved goodbye to the housekeeper and started her car, heading into town. Her first stop was to the florist, to return her vases and stands. A portly, gregarious man, he insisted on calling his wife, she had made a stunning pottery platter for Millie and Sam to celebrate their engagement, and she wanted to give it to Millie now so that they could both enjoy it over Christmas. Millie was speechless, tears welling up in her eyes, the weight of her lie forming a lump in her throat.

It was a similar story at the caterers, the music shop, the bakery, and even more mortifying for Millie, at Rachel's coffee shop, her mum flying out of the kitchen, tears streaming down her face, overjoyed for Millie. Millie wished that the floor would open up and swallow her whole. She couldn't look anyone in the eye, mumbling an excuse about needing to get back home, and agreeing to come for lunch the following day. Fleeing to the safety of her car, Millie slammed the door, locking it for good measure. She was a fraud. A liar. A charlatan. She was no better than her mother, a thought that sobered her. This had to stop. Now. Millie couldn't do this anymore, she couldn't stand next to her dearest friends and work colleagues and blatantly lie to them. There was only one thing that she could do. Shifting her car into gear, she headed for Sam's house.

Pulling into Sam's driveway, Millie noticed an unfamiliar car parked out the front. Sam had company, maybe she should come back later? No, she dismissed the thought, this needed to happen now, before she lost her nerve, before he talked her into waiting. Besides, it would be better with an audience, wouldn't it? That way there was no chance of emotion, or lust, overtaking them. Walking around the side of the house, Millie let herself in through the back door.

"Sam, seriously, you really need to start locking your do-". Millie stopped in her tracks, jaw falling open at the sight of Amanda, naked, in Sam's house. "What the hell!?"

"Oops!" Amanda's hand flew up to cover her mouth, a giggle escaping. "Sammy told me you were out, he said that we would have the house to ourselves today...Wait. What are you doing here?"

"What am I doing here? What the hell are you doing here? And where is Sam?" Millie was so livid she couldn't see straight. Amanda was here, in Sam's house, naked. He had better have a darn good reason for this to ever be acceptable.

"Sam? Oh, he's in the shower right now." A wave of her perfectly manicured hand dismissed Millie's question. "My, my, you do look surprised. Surely you can't be serious? You must have known that Sammy and I are, what did he call us," she paused, putting a finger on her lip as if she was thinking, "oh yes, that's right, fuck buddies." She looked Millie right in the eye. "Did you seriously not guess anything? Even at the Christmas party? Honey, he couldn't take his eyes off me! Why do you think he was so okay with you refusing to go to bed with him? Because I was waiting two doors over, that's why." Amanda gloated, an indulgent smile on her face.

"I don't believe you." Millie's voice sounded flat, even to her own ears, doubt creeping in. How did she know that Sam hadn't slept with her that night?

"Molly, isn't it?" Amanda didn't wait for a reply. "I know all about your contract with Sam, about your fake engagement, he told me everything. He chose you to pretend to be his fiancé as you are bland enough to please his mother and her high standards. He chose me for his lover as I excite him in a way you never could. Why else would he call me first thing this morning? Right after you left his bed, you did sleep with him last night, didn't you? It is written all over your face. Oh, you poor thing, you didn't actually think that it meant anything, did you? I was caught up at work, you were a means to an end, a way to scratch an itch until I could get here. Judging by his insatiable hunger for me today, you weren't that good at scratching." Amanda barked out a laugh at Millie's expense. "This shower is the first time he hasn't been buried inside me since this morning. Mmm, I ache in all the right places." Millie refused to rise to the bait, instead, walking across to the kitchen bench where her signed contract sat for all to see.

Picking it up in her hands, Millie tore it into two pieces, turning it and tearing it again, dropping the pieces onto the kitchen bench.

"Amanda, do me a favour? Please let Sam know that I stopped by, to put an end to this. Whatever game he is playing, he can play alone, I am not interested. I won't lie to my friends. I'm out." She looked over at Amanda, lifting her chin slightly, determined not to allow the other woman to see how hurt she was. "Goodbye Amanda, I hope you end up getting whatever it is that you really want." Millie almost choked on her words, turning on her heel, walking out of the back door with her head held high.

CHAPTER FIFTEEN

Sam turned off the shower and strained to listen. He thought that he had heard...Millie! He smiled at the thought of her, he had ached for her all day, not wanting to disturb her, knowing that she had a busy day ahead. Instead, he had pottered about at home, waiting, knowing that she would eventually come home, to him. Wrapping a towel around his waist, he padded down the stairs, his grin fading at the sight that greeted him. Amanda was standing in his kitchen, facing the back door, completely naked, hand raised, fingers waving goodbye. Sam barely caught a glance at Millie's face before she had turned, marching down the driveway towards her car, shoulders squared, stride determined. What he had seen sent shivers down his spine. A look of confusion, of resignation, on Millie's face, and worse, much, much worse, the single tear he saw fall from her eye before she had time to blink it away.

"Millie." The name had no sooner left his lips than he was catapulted backwards, Amanda having launched herself at him, her arms a vice around his neck.

"What the hell?"

"Sammy, oh, it was terrible! She attacked me! Thank goodness you are here." Sam regained his footing, pushing Amanda off of him, striding out the back door just in time to see Millie's car scream around the corner, headed for town. He started for his car, stopping, remembering that he was in a towel, heading back to the house to change.

"Amanda, you have two minutes to explain to me exactly why you are in my house, and why you are naked. And get some damn clothes on!"

"What am I doing here? Sammy, I came here for you, for us." She advanced towards him. "I saw the way you looked at me at the Christmas party, it was obvious you wanted me. So here I am," she stopped in front of him, "your Christmas gift."

"And this is yours. You're fired. You have two minutes to get dressed and leave my house before I have you arrested with breaking and entering and trespassing."

"Sammy, you don't mean that." Amanda started. "Mollie's gone anyway; you won't get her back you know." Amanda gloated.

"What did you say to her?" Sam rounded on Amanda; anger evident in his voice.

"I just told her a few home truths, Sammy, that's all. Face it, you and I are meant to be together. Why else would I still be working for you?"

"Amanda, firstly, you no longer work for me, I just fired you. Secondly, the only reason that I kept you on for so long is because your father is a dear friend of mine. If he had any idea of what you had done here today..." Sam trailed off, his intention clear.

"Sam, you can't seriously be thinking of telling him, please! I'm sorry, it won't happen again."

"You're right, it won't. Tell me what else you told Millie."

"I saw your engagement contract on the counter, I called her out on it. I told her that you had only chosen her to please your mother and her high standards, but that I was the one who set you on fire."

"You let her think that we had sex, here, today?" Sam honestly could not believe that Amanda would do such a thing.

"Yes."

"Why? What on earth did I ever do to you?"

"Nothing Sam, you did nothing. You didn't even notice me, not once!" Amanda's voice shook. Sam shook his head, baffled that someone would go to such lengths just to be noticed.

"What did Millie say when you told her these lies?" Millie would have known they were lies, wouldn't she? Sam wasn't so sure.

"She ripped the contract up, told me to let you know that she was done."

"Get dressed, Amanda. I won't tell your father, and I won't involve the police, on one condition. You leave this house, and you hand in your resignation. I don't want to see your face ever again, is that clear?"

"Yes." Sam turned, marching up to his room to throw on some clothes. By the time he came back downstairs, Amanda was gone. He looked at the ripped up contract on the bench, anger stirring inside. Millie had obviously believed Amanda's story, why else would she have ripped up the contract? Sam wasn't sure what made him angrier, the fact that Millie had believed Amanda without question, or the fact that she had backed out of their agreement. He stewed it over on the drive over to Millie's house, tearing into her driveway at breakneck speed, screeching to a stop inches from her house. He stormed up to the front door, banging on it with his fist, his anger bubbling over.

"Millie, open the door, I know you are home." He banged again, waiting. "Millie!"

The door opened a crack, the safety chain still firmly on. "Millie, let me in, we need to talk."

"Go away Sam, I don't want to talk to you." She was amazed at how steady her voice could sound, even when she was trembling inside.

"Well, that's too bad, because I have something that I want to say to you." He wedged his foot in the door, making it impossible for Millie to fully close the door. "I didn't sleep with Amanda, not today, not ever."

"Fine." The single syllable was all that she could manage.

"You don't believe me?" Sam sounded surprised.

"I don't care either way." Millie clarified with a lie.

"Well, I do, dammit!" Sam slammed his hand on the door in frustration.

"Fine, if you must know, no, I don't believe you, Amanda knew...things, things she couldn't know otherwise." Millie knew that she sounded resigned, in a way, maybe she was.

"So, you're telling me that you are willing to give up two million dollars, on the word of Amanda?" Now it was Sam's turn to sound incredulous.

"No, I am giving up the two million dollars because it is the right thing to do. I wouldn't expect you to understand that Sam, it probably comes as a second nature to you, lying, but for me, not so much. I won't lie to my friends anymore, it isn't right."

"I see. Just who is lying now, Millie?"

"What do you mean?"

"You were ever so happy to lie before Amanda came on the scene, and now, suddenly, you have higher morals."

Millie looked at the ring on her finger, unable to bear its weight anymore. It all started as a bit of a joke, a lark, no one was supposed to get hurt, least of all her. Yet that is exactly what had happened. Somewhere along the line she forgot that this ring wasn't really hers to wear, she forgot that she was only meant to be playing a part, and instead she started making plans. She had been foolish, stupid even, and now she was paying the price. In more ways than one. She looked around the entryway of her house. She would lose all of this, and for what? Her pride? Her heart? Could she change her mind? Could she go on pretending that she was engaged to Sam, even after everything that they had shared? He was completely unaffected, he obviously felt nothing for her. Staying would mean ripping her heart wide open with every passing second. No, she would survive losing the house, probably, but she wouldn't survive losing Sam, not if she stayed any longer. She wrenched the ring off her finger, shoving it through the door towards Sam, dropping it into his open hand.

"Take it, I'm done."

"Millie!"

"Goodbye Sam." With a might push, Millie shoved the door close, twisting the deadbolt into place. Millie stood, head leaning against the front door for what seemed like eons, her heart shattering into a million pieces, hot tears falling freely down her face. It wasn't until she heard Sam's car start and drive away that she moved, numbly, as if in a trance, upstairs to her bedroom, not bothering to strip off before climbing fully clothed under her sheets, curling into a ball as sobs wracked her body.

Sam drove home on autopilot, sitting in his car in his driveway for so long that his neighbour tapped on the window to check if he was okay. Shaking himself from his fog, Sam went inside, wandering aimlessly, unable to settle. He poured himself a shot of whiskey, taking it out on the back patio, mulling over the day's events. Millie had been a fool to turn down the two million dollars, he was certain of it. All she had to do was put up with him for a few more days and she would have saved her property. He would like to pretend that he doesn't care if she wants to throw the money away or not, but he does care. She will lose her home. Something nags at his conscious. It was all his fault, he should never had slept with her, no matter how tempting she had been, how tempting she still was, even angry at him all he wanted to do was make love to her. He had never felt that way before, not ever. He wondered why he felt that way now, with Millie? Heck, she was his best friend's sister, she was off limits.

If Josh found out about this, it could well end their friendship, a sobering thought. It surprised Sam that he wasn't more upset about his friendship with Josh, instead, he was more worried about Millie. What on earth had gotten into him? They grew up together for heaven's sake! Apart from that one crazy teenage infatuation, Sam had barely thought about Millie. Liar, his mind whispered. Good grief! Had his father been right all along? Could he have been avoiding Millie this whole time? Protecting his feelings from getting hurt? His chest tightened painfully; he knew it was true. He had avoided her over the years for one blinding reason. He loved her, still loved her, more than that, he was in love with her. And he had ruined everything.

Sam couldn't breathe, his heart was pounding, his ears ringing. He had to fix this, he had to. He couldn't just let Millie walk away from him, he couldn't. The only problem was, he had no idea how to. He would give her the money for the house if only she would let him, but he knew she never would, she would simply find some way of returning it to him. He wondered just how opposed Millie would be to one more lie, a plan starting to form in his head. There was just one thing that Sam needed, and for that, he would have to get his parents on board, which meant that he would need to come clean about his deception. Sam knew that for Millie, he would do anything.

CHAPTER SIXTEEN

When Millie finally dragged herself from bed the following day, she felt better able to face the world, no matter what it would entail. She didn't need Sam, or any other man for that matter, to fix her problems, no, she could do it on her own. Fortified with a strong black coffee, Millie dressed in a smart casual dress, and headed into town, determination etched on her face. Millie's meeting with the bank manager went about as well as she had expected it to. Although he was kind enough, it didn't lessen the hardness of the meeting. With a final signature, Millie relinquished all rights to her grandfather's property and estate. Millie paused, pen in mid-air, before drawing in a deep breath, squaring her shoulders, placing the pen carefully down on this island paperwork, pushing it all across the desk to the bank manager.

Millie's resolve was strong, she would not cry, not here in any case, maybe later tonight, in the privacy of her bedroom, she would howl at the unfairness of life, and grieve for all that she had lost, but not now, not in public. No, in public she would be strong and calm, giving no indication to the swirling emotions beneath the surface. With a final nod at the bank manager, Millie left, stepping out into the bright sun and the bustling Main Street of Maitland, full of shoppers dashing this way and that, eager to snap up a last-minute Christmas gift. There were a lot of tourists in town for Christmas, the Christmas markets were taking place today and tomorrow, which were always a popular attraction for homemade delicacies. Millie wondered briefly if Sam would bring Amanda into town, then decided that was a train of thought best not explored.

Millie trailed along, wandering aimlessly, swept up in the crowds. She paused at a stall selling macarons, buying a box of intricately decorated Christmas ones for Josh, who had always loved macarons. Even the fact that Josh would be home later today did nothing to lift Millie's spirits. Not ready to go home just yet, not that it was home anymore, not really, Millie walked a bit further, browsing through a used book stall and making a couple of purchases.

Deciding to make a nice lamb roast for Josh for dinner, Millie stepped into the local butcher's, crowded with customers ordering their Christmas seafood. Millie froze in the doorway, Sam's intent gaze meeting hers from across the room. Without a word Millie spun on her heel and left, if she had to speak to him, it would be the final straw that tipped her over the edge today, and that was a risk that she was not willing to take. Once Millie was safely in her car, she allowed herself to relax, exhaling the deep breath she didn't realise that she had been holding, feeling her shoulders slump.

Millie was busy scrubbing the kitchen floor on her hands and knees when Josh walked through the door, as tall as a reed, looking every bit the larrikin Millie knew that he was. She couldn't stop the tears that welled in her eyes, so happy she was to see her brother. He embraced her in a bear hug, refusing to let go until her tears had subsided.

"Millie, what's wrong?"

"Nothing, not really, I have just missed you so much." Millie sniffed loudly, embarrassed. "I'm so glad you're here for Christmas." She hugged him tightly before releasing him again.

"Are you hungry? I can fix an early dinner if you like?"

"No, I, ah, stopped off at The Daily Grind, Rachel fixed me something already." A slight blush appeared on Josh's ears. Interesting.

"Okay, well, there is a box of macarons on the table for you whenever you like."

"That's sis, I might go sit on the patio, watch the world go by." Millie grinned as he swiped the box of macarons on his way past, he really did have the most dreadful sweet tooth.

"I'll just finish up here and then join you." Millie smiled. "There is something that I want to talk to you about." She turned her attention back to the floor, scrubbing half-heartedly. Deciding the floor was clean enough, Millie dropped the scrubbing brush into the bucket of water and stood, stretching her muscles out as she went. She could hear the telephone ringing, heard Josh answer it, before calling her name, appearing in the kitchen, and holding the telephone out to her.

"It's the bank."

"Thank you." Millie took the telephone from Josh, slipping past him into the study, closing the door firmly behind her. She wasn't sure how much information the bank had told Josh, but until she had spoken to him personally, she did not want him overhearing her conversation. "Hello, this is Millie."

"Millie, it's Brian Howard, bank manager."

"Yes, Brian."

"I have good news, we have a buyer for your property, already pre-approved for purchase, so we won't be needing to go to auction after all."

"Wow, that was fast." Millie tried to sound upbeat, she knew it wasn't the bank managers fault that she was in this position, he had been more than kind to her, and securing a sale, especially this fast, in this market, was a small miracle.

"Best of all Millie, they aren't interested in subdividing, they want it to remain as is."

"That's great, thank you!"

"I know it isn't the outcome you initially hoped for Millie, and I'm sorry for that. The new owners want to remain anonymous, and they are in no hurry to take possession of the property. They are happy for you to remain as long as you need, rent-free, in exchange for keeping an eye on the place."

"Thank you, Brian, I appreciate that, but it is unnecessary. I shall be vacating the property on the twenty-eight of December. I will leave the keys in the letterbox."

"Okay Millie, I will let the new owners know. If I don't see you before you leave, I hope you have a very Merry Christmas Millie, and best of luck with everything in the future." Brian ended the call. Millie, reluctant to join Josh on the patio, and have to explain the situation, lingered in the study a moment longer. Tomorrow was Christmas Eve; how merry could it be?

"Josh, can we talk for a moment please?" Millie slumped down in one of the patio chairs opposite Josh.

"Is this about the bank?" Josh set his newspaper aside.

"Yes."

"Go on, I'm listening." Millie spent the better part of the next hour explaining to Josh the situation that she had found herself in, how their grandfather had hidden the second mortgage from them, how it had come due and there had been no other option but to sell. She purposely left out the entire debacle with Sam, there was no need for Josh to know about that, it would serve no purpose now, other than to turn Josh against Sam, and Millie had no intention of letting that happen. Instead, she stuck to facts and left all emotion out of it.

"Wow, I can't even begin to fathom...You said that we will be out by the twenty-eight of December?"

"Yes." Millie nodded.

"Millie, are you sure that you are okay with this," concern laced Josh's voice, "you seem very calm about everything, I mean, you literally have a matter of days before you need to walk away from this place, where will you go?"

"I'm fine Josh, really," Millie lied, something which was becoming a bit of a habit for her lately. "I'm going to make a fresh start, in Sydney, if you'll let me stay with you for a few days."

"What?! You're going to leave Maitland? You love this place; you have always said that this is home for you."

"I did, didn't I? well, I can't stay in the same place forever Josh, hiding away, sooner or later I need to start acting like a grown-up, you know, a proper job, a house, a dog." Millie ticked things off on her fingers.

"Millie, is there something that you aren't telling me? Has something happened between you and Rachel?"

"No," Millie breathed a sigh of relief, "Rachel and I are fine, I promise. There is nothing here for me Josh, not anymore. I'm ready for a new start, I need one. Now come on, stop worrying so much big brother, and embrace the adventure." Millie was saved from having to explain anymore by the arrival of a car, an all too familiar car, colour staining her cheeks at just how familiar the car was for her. "You have a visitor." Millie couldn't help the venom that tainted her words.

"Millie, be nice."

"Don't worry brother dear, as far as your friend goes," she refused to say his name, "I'm always nice." Millie stood. "Excuse me, I'm going for a walk. Nice does not mean that I have to be entertaining." With that, Millie headed back through the house, ignoring the eyes that she could feel following her all the way from his car.

CHAPTER SEVENTEEN

Sam watched Millie walk away angrily, his heart aching. He wondered what Josh and Millie had been discussing when he drove up, he wondered if Josh knew about the arrangement that Sam had had with Millie. He was about to find out.

"Josh!" Sam greeted him enthusiastically, clapping him on the shoulder and ushering him up onto the patio. "Would you like a beer mate?"

"Thanks." Sam took the proffered bottle of beer, opening it and taking a large swig. "Is, ah, Millie here?"

"Millie?" Josh's brows knitted together. "No, she's gone for a walk."

"She's angry with me."

"No, she's just...What do you mean she's angry with you? Why would she be angry with you?" Josh fixed Sam with a hard stare. "Sam, is there something going on here that I should know about?"

"Has she told you about the house?" Sam tested the waters, not sure how much Millie had already revealed to Josh.

"Yes. She's pretending like she's fine of course, but something's wrong, I've never seen her like this before. Can you believe that she told me she has no intention of staying in Maitland?"

"What?!" Sam's head shot up, as did his heart rate. Millie was leaving? "Did she tell you the whole story Josh, including our little arrangement?"

"I asked her if there was anything else going on, she said no. I had a feeling that she was hiding something from me, and apparently, that is something that you know about, is that right Sam?"

"Yes, I need to let you know about something, I'm just not sure where to start."

"I would suggest at the beginning."

Sam leant back in his chair, and started at the beginning, telling Josh about how Millie had confided in him about the fact that they were in danger of losing their grandfathers property, how she had asked him for help, financially. Sam told Josh about his

170

counteroffer, about asking Millie to pretend to be his fiancé over the Christmas period, how he had asked her out of desperation, wanting to avoid his mother's matchmaking attempts. Sam assured Josh that everything had been aboveboard, it had been a legitimate business deal, they had used a proper contract, which they had both signed. Lastly, Sam told Josh the truth, that he had screwed up, that he had been stupid, and Millie had ripped up the contract and had refused to speak to him ever since.

"Seriously Sam, that does sound pretty stupid, but hardly a reason for her to hate you. Maybe you misunderstood?"

"No." Sam was adamant. "There's more. I let things get out of hand, I let the fake engagement go too far, and then there was the whole Amanda debacle."

"Who the heck is Amanda?"

"An ex-employee. She showed up at my place, naked mind you, and when Millie showed up, Amanda convinced her that she and I were having an affair."

"So what? It was a fake engagement, why should Millie care?"

"It was the wedding, the lines became very blurry, Millie and I, well, we had a fling." The mumbled words had barely left Sam's mouth before he found himself flat on the floor, his chair toppled sideways, a smarting pain making its way through his jaw. "Ouch! What the heck?!"

"You jerkoff! You took advantage of my sister!" Josh reached down and hauled him up by the scruff of his shirt, pinning him to the wall of the house, his face contorted with rage. "If I were you, I would think very carefully about the next words out of your mouth, if you want to avoid being thrown back down in the dirt."

"Josh, it wasn't like that, I swear it wasn't. I mean," he took a deep breath, releasing it slowly, "I love her," he choked out, "I'm in love with her, maybe I always was." The look of anger on Josh's face disappeared, replaced instead with one of utmost surprise. He dropped his hands to his sides, releasing Sam from the wall, flopping down in his chair.

"You love her. Millie. You are in love with Millie, with my sister." Josh whispered, a smile stretching across his face.

"I am, but you needn't look so pleased, she hates my guts right now," Sam said miserably, sitting back down in his chair opposite Josh.

"Yeah, interesting that, don't you think?" Josh smirked over at his friend.

"What do you mean?"

"When we would hang out as kids, she was completely indifferent to you and your existence, you were pretty much another piece of furniture. She didn't like you."

"Okay, is there a point in there?"

"She didn't like you Sam, yet she didn't care two hoots if you were hanging around or not, it was of no consequence to her. Now she seems to be avoiding you like the plague. You claim that she hates you, but I think that you are wrong. I think that you will find that her feelings are in fact the opposite. She loves you."

"You really think so?" Sam tried not to look too hopeful.

"Of course. If she really hated you, she wouldn't care if you were hanging around or not. Trust me on this, you two are perfect for each other."

"I hope you're right."

"I am," Josh grinned, "now all you need to do is to convince her of this."

"Actually, I have a plan on how to do that, but I am going to need your help, that is, if you will give me your permission to see your sister," Sam asked, no longer certain about Josh's answer.

"Sam, you are my best friend. It would be an absolute honour to have you join this family, if that is what Millie wants. If it isn't, well," Josh shrugged, "well, you are still my best friend, that will never change."

Relieved, Sam held out his hand, the two men shaking, their friendship firm, their earlier altercation already forgotten. Sam filled Josh in on his plan, and while tempted to linger, decided against it. As much as Sam ached to see Millie, he knew that now was not the time, he would wait one more day, he wanted his plan to be perfect for Millie, she deserved that, she deserved perfect.

CHAPTER EIGHTEEN

By the time Millie returned from her walk, the house was quiet. She found Josh sitting at the kitchen table, a recipe book open in front of him.

"Has your friend gone?" Millie sat down in the chair next to Josh.

"You know, he has a name, Millie." Josh smiled at her.

"Fine." Millie rolled her eyes childishly. "Has Sam gone?"

"Yes." Millie nodded. "Aren't you curious as to why he came over?" Josh prodded. A chill snaked down Millie's spine. Surely not. Sam would never tell Josh, would he?

"Not really." Millie lied. "I assumed that he was here for the same reason that he is always here, to catch up with you." Millie squirmed under Josh's unrelenting gaze. "What?" She questioned, hoping that she did not sound as defensive as she felt.

"Nothing, you are just looking a little bit red in the face there, sister dear, I hope you're not getting sick, what a horrid way to spend Christmas."

"I'm fine, I probably just overexerted myself on my walk, that's all." Millie placated. "So, what are you looking at?"

"I'm thinking of trying to make a three-tiered meringue and chocolate mousse cake for dessert for Christmas Eve, decorated with meringue kisses and macarons, what do you think?"

"Christmas Eve is tomorrow." Millie reminded him.

"I know that."

"Okay, well, I think a dessert like that will take you all day to make and to be honest, it is a bit of overkill for the two of us, don't you think?"

"Hmm. Oh, it won't just be for the two of us Millie, didn't I tell you?"

"Tell me what?" dread started to form in the pit of Millie's stomach.

"Sam's parents have invited us to spend Christmas Eve night with them."

"What?!" Millie shot out of her chair. "Are you serious?"

"Yes, of course, why? Is something wrong?"

"No, I...I..." Millie could no longer form words, her mouth flapped open and shut like a fish. "I'm just surprised is all, were you going to ask me about this, or is it already a done deal?"

"I'm sorry Millie, I didn't think it was something that I would have to ask you about, I had no idea that you would have any issues with it. Did you have other plans?"

"No, not really. I just thought that it would be the two of us, seeing as how it is going to be our last Christmas in this house."

"Millie." Josh eyed her, a serious expression on his face. "If it makes it easier for you, the invitation came from Kathy and John, not from Sam. They have always been kind to us, and anyway, it isn't just us that they have invited. Sam tells me that they have asked Rachel to join us, along with a couple of other local friends."

"What time are we expected to be there?"

"From five o'clock in the afternoon onwards."

"Fine." Millie looked down at the recipe book in front of Josh. "If I were you I would use fresh strawberries, not macarons, they are Rachel's favourite." She winked at Josh.

"I'll think about it." He muttered, not quite meeting her gaze. Millie drifted off to make a start on dinner, not at all inspired. She thickly sliced a cob loaf, lightly toasting the pieces. She made a plate of fried egg, bacon, sizzle steak, sliced tomato, lettuce, and cheese sandwiches, placing it in front of Josh at the table. "This looks delicious Millie, thank you!"

"You're welcome. Do you need any help?" Millie gestured to the recipe book.

"No, thank you, I kinda want to do this myself."

Millie spent the rest of the evening perched on a barstool at the kitchen bench, keeping Josh company as he attempted to make his three-tiered meringue and chocolate mousse cake decorated with meringue kisses and fresh strawberries. It was not a particularly successful endeavour, and eventually, Millie was forced to call it a night, leaving Josh alone to battle on in the kitchen, she crawled into bed just after midnight. When Millie came downstairs the following morning, Christmas Eve, the place resembled a rubbish dump. Dirty dishes littered the kitchen from one end to the other, rubbish piled up in the sink, and there were tea towels everywhere. There was, however, no sign of Josh. Millie tentatively opened the fridge, not quite sure what she would find inside, a gasp of surprise escaping at the sight that greeted her. There, taking pride of place, was a three-tiered meringue and chocolate mousse cake decorated with meringue kisses and fresh strawberries. Slightly wonky, and not exactly uniform, it was gorgeous. Josh had actually done it.

Deciding that he had earnt a sleep in, Millie poured herself a coffee, donned a pair of thick rubber gloves, and got to work tidying up the kitchen. When Josh did finally emerge, it was mid-afternoon, and the place was spotless. Millie, too pent up to do nothing, had single-handedly boxed up the entire downstairs. The house and property had been sold as is, the only exception being anything that Millie or Josh owned outright, which was not a whole lot. Millie's chest ached with the weight of the burden. She knew it was her fault that Josh was losing half of his inheritance, although he said otherwise when she told him yesterday, she knew he was upset at the prospect. If only she had been braver, or stronger maybe, maybe then she could have remained engaged to Sam, remained locked into his contract. Sure, it would have cost her her soul, but at least she would have saved the property. Her eyes were raw with unshed tears, as she shoved a last stack of paperwork into the box, sealing it up, before carting it over to the back door and stacking it with the rest of the boxes there.

Everything in this house was someone else's now, Millie wondered what they would do with it all. She highly doubted that the new owner would want her grandfather's collection of rusted fishing lures, or the shed full of junk and broken-down appliances, which her grandfather had always insisted might be useful one day. It was a strange feeling for Millie, standing there, in a home so familiar, surrounded by everything that she knew, all the while knowing that everything was different. She had packed away all of her grandfather's paperwork, and photographs, and had added her meagre few belongings to the boxes as well, only leaving out the bare necessities, those items which she thought that she would need over the next couple of days. It was interesting, Millie thought, or maybe just plain sad, to see just how few boxes there were, after living in this home for as long as they had. Eight boxes. That was all that it amounted to.

When Josh came to find her, Millie was busy moving the packed boxes from the back door across to the shed, where they would be easier to pack into the car ready to move.

"Millie! You're not even dressed yet." Josh shook his head softly, a look of disappointment on his face.

"Is it that time already? I'm sorry, I didn't realise. I'll just run upstairs and change really quick; I won't be a moment." Millie flew upstairs, and straight into the shower, finishing in record speed. Towelling off, she rummaged around in her wardrobe until she found what she was looking for, the perfect outfit, three quarter length jeans and a shapeless, oversized Christmas tee shirt. Paired with red ballet flats, her outfit was comfortable, yet not too bland. As an added bonus, it was not at all attractive, there was absolutely no way that Millie was going to give Sam a chance to look at her ever again. She ran a brush through her hair, slicked on clear lip balm, and re-joined Josh downstairs. He raised his eyebrows at her appearance but wisely kept his mouth shut. He might want to dress up in a suit, but Millie preferred to be comfortable.

They turned into Sam's parents' driveway right behind Rachel, but even knowing that her best friend was here did nothing to quell the churning storm inside Millie's stomach. She shoved her left hand inside her pocket, and reluctantly got out of the car, determinedly ignoring Kathy and John and Sam, who were all standing at the front door waving. While Josh went straight over, hugging Kathy and greeting John, Millie turned towards Rachel, quickly pulling her over, turning them both away from the prying eyes on the front patio.

"Rachel, quick." Millie started an urgent tone to her voice. "Long story short. I slept with Sam." Millie ignored Rachel's gasp. "We had a huge fight, I broke off the fake engagement, and I sold my grandfather's property. I'm moving to Sydney with Josh on the twenty-eighth of December. Oh, and Kathy and John have no idea."

Millie looked at her friend, Rachel's mouth was hanging open, and she was blinking rapidly.

"You're leaving?" She whispered. Millie only nodded, afraid that if she spoke, she would start crying, and if that happened, she might not stop.

"Millie, Rachel, what could be so fascinating as to keep you over there?" Kathy called out. Millie looked at Rachel, her eyes asking a question.

"We're coming," Rachel called back, then more softly, so that only Millie could hear, "we'll talk about his later, okay? There is no way I'm giving you up without a fight." Rachel looped her arm through Millie's, and heads together, the two friends walked up to the house.

"Millie." Kathy stopped her with a hand. "You look lovely tonight."

'Thank you," Millie squirmed. "I apologise for not getting dressed up Kathy, I had no desire to tonight." Was that a smirk she saw litter across Sam's face? With a bit of luck, he'll choke on his dinner.

"Millie, may I speak to you for a moment please?"

"Um, sure." Rachel shrugged to Millie as she followed everyone else into the house.

"Please, take your hand out of your pocket, you don't need to hide it from me, Sam has already confessed."

"He has?" Now, this was a surprise. Millie had thought that Sam would simply ignore the situation, or maybe even lie about it.

"He feels terrible, actually we all do. I just wanted to let you know that I don't want you feeling bad, we have all played pranks in our day, haven't we?"

"I guess so."

"Good, now, let's eat, I don't know about you Millie, but I am starving!"

CHAPTER NINETEEN

Dinner was actually a lot nicer than Millie had expected it to be. She had dreaded it, had thought that it would be unbearably awkward, and instead, she had almost enjoyed it. Kathy had gone to so much effort, the table was arranged beautifully, with an abundance of poinsettia and greenery, small glass baubles used as place settings, hand-lettered in gold. John and Kathy sat at opposite ends, with Josh and Sam on one side, and Millie and Rachel on the other side, with Millie opposite Sam. Millie refused to look at Sam, if he asked her a question, she answered cordially enough, her eyes firmly on her plate. The conversation centred around safe topics, Josh mostly, and his work in the army. Eventually, though, talk turned to the new year, and Millie casually mentioned that she would be returning to Sydney with Josh.

"Millie, are you sure?" Kathy asked gently.

"Absolutely certain." Millie nodded, not a trace of hesitation in her voice. It was amazing really, how much one could start believing something if they just repeated to themselves again and again and again.

"It will be a nice change." Millie smiled at the table full of faces in front of her. "I'm thinking that I might go back to university."

"Oh, that's wonderful dear." Kathy reached over and patted Millie's hand. "What will you study?"

"Teaching," Millie answered automatically. "It is a pretty versatile degree, if I ever decide to travel overseas, it might come in handy."

"I didn't know you wanted to travel, Millie," Sam spoke up.

"Well, that's hardly surprising is it Sam? After all, you barely know me." Millie threw caution to the wind, looking Sam directly in the eye and giving him a saccharine sweet smile.

"No." He held her gaze, unblinking, for several seconds, before replying. "I guess not." Millie couldn't explain it, but she suddenly felt ice-cold, her insides felt like they had been turned to sludge. Millie dropped her eyes to her plate, breathing slowly, trying not to let Sam see just how much his comment had affected her.

Josh's three-tiered meringue and chocolate mousse cake, decorated with meringue kisses and fresh strawberries, was a huge hit. Millie alone ate two slices, and she would have had a third, had it not been for the smug way that Sam was watching her, an all too kissable look on his face. After the last of the dinner dishes had been cleared away, Rachel made her excuses to leave, her own family would be expecting her. She left Millie with a hug, and a promise to call her tomorrow to catch up on all of her news. Millie wished that she had some excuse to leave, instead, she allowed herself to be drawn into a conversation with Kathy, who had recently acquired a Victorian-era dollhouse, that she was hoping to restore to its original condition. Millie was all too happy to follow her upstairs to her craft room to have a look, the dollhouse even more magnificent than Kathy had described. When they returned downstairs, Millie found only Sam in the lounge room.

"Where is everyone?" Kathy asked, looking around the room as if they would suddenly appear.

"Dad's gone upstairs," Sam replied with an indulgent smile. "I think Josh's dessert did him in."

"And Josh?"

"He left." Sam folded the newspaper he had been reading in half, and laid it on the coffee table.

"What?" Millie couldn't believe it. Josh had left her, here.

"Don't worry dear," Kathy misunderstood Millie's distress, "Sam will drive you home, won't you dear?"

"It would be my...pleasure." The slight pause in his sentence made Millie nervous, she remembered all too well what had happened the last time they had been alone in a car together, and she had no intention of allowing that to happen again.

"I would rather walk," Millie muttered beneath her breath.

"What dear?"

"Nothing Kathy, that's very kind," Millie said goodbye to Kathy in the loungeroom, aware that this would be the last time that she would likely see the other woman. Kathy made Millie promise that she would keep in touch, that she would send Kathy a card from time to time so that she knew that Millie was okay. Millie was all too happy to agree to her simple request. Sam held the front door open for Millie as she stalked past him, not stopping and not slowing, all the way down the driveway and out onto the street. Sam caught up to Millie as she crossed the street, grabbing her by the elbow and yanking her back.

"What the heck do you think you're doing Millie? I said I would drive you home, now get into the car."

"Get your hands off me!" Millie wrenched her arm free. "I said that I would walk, so," she shooed him with her hands, "off you go, run on home. I'm sure Amanda must be well-rested by now." Millie turned angrily on her heel and started to march away.

"Millie." Sam jogged in front of her, blocking her path. "What did she say to you?"

"Seriously? Like it matters?" Millie stopped and looked at him. "She told me the truth Sam, which is more than you ever did. Tell me, did lying always come so naturally to you, or did you have to practice it?"

"I didn't sleep with Amanda." Sam hissed.

"I don't care who you sleep with."

"Really? You don't? Then why so upset when you saw Amanda at my house? Why not simply sit down and have coffee while you waited for me? I'll tell you why Millie, because you were jealous."

"You wish Sam." Millie refuted his claims.

"Tell me, Millie, what was it exactly that made you so mad? Was it the fact that it was Amanda? Or maybe that she was naked? You see," Sam stepped closer to Millie, "I think it was because she told you we had been together, and the thought of me touching her, well, it was too much for your little green monster to take, wasn't it? After all, if I am going to touch anybody, it should be you." Sam ended in a whisper. He reached his hand out towards Millie, and gently cupped her face. The sound of Millie's palm connecting with Sam's face reverberated through the air.

"Don't touch me!" Millie seethed, her palm smarting, mortification flooding her face.

"You, my darling, just proved my point." Sam grinned at her, rubbing his cheek with his hand.

"Really? What point is that?" Millie bit out. "The fact that you are an ars-" Sam placed a finger on her lips, silencing her.

"I wouldn't want you saying anything that you might regret Millie. Especially considering that you are in love with me."

"I, what?!" Croaked Millie, her voice rising several notches.

"You are in love with me, it is obvious." Sam's voice was confident.

"You're insane." Millie refuted, but her heart wasn't in it. She was tired, she was emotionally exhausted, and she did not want to stand outside arguing with Sam all night.

"It is just as well," Sam continued as if he hadn't heard her speak, "considering that I am in love with you." Millie stared at him for a long moment before turning away and walking away from him. "Millie, please." It was the sound of the ache in Sam's voice that stopped Millie. "Please hear me out."

"Fine." Millie turned back around but didn't move any closer to Sam. "No more lies Sam, I want the truth."

"I love you, Millie, I am in love with you. I don't know when it happened, maybe it was always there, maybe my teenage infatuation wasn't just an infatuation, at least that is what my father seems to think anyway."

"You told your father?" Millie was stunned, and maybe a little impressed.

"Of course, the moment I left your house the other day, I drove straight to my parents' house and told them everything. I told them that I had stuffed up, that I hadn't told you I loved you when I had the chance, that I had lost you."

"Sam." Millie shook her head sadly, wanting so desperately to believe him.

"Millie," Sam closed the distance between them, "how could you ever think that I would even so much as look at another woman, let alone anything else?" This time when he reached out for her, Millie let him, his hand cupping her face, his thumb wiping away a tear Millie hadn't realised was falling. "When I have everything I ever dreamed of right here?" Sam lowered his face towards Millie's, slowly, giving her plenty of time to push him away. His lips met hers with a sweetness that had her aching for more, gentle, his tongue exploring her mouth, cherishing her. It was unlike any other kiss they had shared, it was full of promise and hope, and love.

Millie broke the kiss, looking up at Sam, tears in her eyes.

"Sam, you were right." Her voice was thick with emotion. "I was jealous. I hadn't realised until that day, that I loved you. That is why I was at your house, to tell you. I couldn't wait anymore, I wanted you to know." This time when Sam kissed her it was full of longing and need, and a burning desire.

"Come home with me Millie?" Sam asked tentatively.

"Yes." Millie's answer was a sigh, a promise, a wish. Sam held the door open for her, kissing her lightly on the forehead before closing the door and getting in on the driver's side. The short drive to Sam's house was silent, both of them lost in their own thoughts. Once inside, there was no preamble, Sam merely took Millie's hand and led her upstairs to his bedroom.

Sam undressed her with reverence, gathering her close to him, to feather kisses along her jawline. Millie tugged at his shirt, and he laughingly moved, stripping his clothes off, before gathering her back in his arms and placing her carefully on the bed as if she were made of glass. Sam's gaze slowly raked over her body. Leaning down, he captured Millie's mouth in a kiss that was so full of love and promise, it left her in no doubt as to his feelings for her. Sam's hand slid down to cup Millie's centre, delight colouring his face at her wetness. With a sigh, he dipped his head to capture her breast, teasing her nipple until it hardened and pebbled beneath his tongue, suckling and biting, Millie moaning in delight. His fingers delved into her silky folds, dipping in and out, causing Millie to writhe beneath him. Sam scooted lower down on the bed, spearing Millie's core with his tongue. Millie's breathing grew hard, she moved her hips in sync with Sam's tongue thrusts, desperate for release. Sam rose to his knees and drove his erection into her, before pulling out fully and driving in again. Millie arched her back and bucked her hips to meet his powerful thrusts, screaming in pleasure as he drove in harder and deeper, his thick member filling her to breaking point, his pelvic bone pressing against her sensitive nub. Millie held nothing back as he moved within her, she was his completely. Pulling his length out fully, he gave one final thrust into her core, her walls tightened around his stiffened member as he pushed her over the edge, screaming his name with wild abandon. With one final thrust he exploded inside her, gripping her hips for support, until totally spent, he collapsed beside her.

Hours later, totally spent, Millie lay in Sam's arms, listening to the sound of his breathing.

"Millie?" Sam sat upright, rummaging around in his bedside table, before turning to face her.

"Hmm."

"Marry me?" He held the ring box out to her. "Marry me, darling?"

"Yes." Millie held out her hand, a look of amazement on her face. Sam slid the ring back onto her finger, her ring, back where it should always have been.

"Is it too early to give you your engagement gift?"

"What? How did you know that I would say yes?" Millie teased.

"I wrote to Santa." Sam joked. "Seriously, I want you to have this now." Sam handed her an envelope.

"Sam!" Millie couldn't believe what she was seeing. "You bought my house?"

"Yes. For you."

"Why?"

"Because it was your grandfather's, and because I love you. Even if you had turned me down flat, I would have still given you the house Millie, no matter how much it hurt to see you again."

"I love you, Sam Marsden," Millie confessed, happily spending the next hour showing him exactly how much she loved him.

EPILOGUE

"Mum, Dad, I'm sorry I'm late, I got caught up. I stopped past and invited Millie and Josh to join us, I hope that's okay?" Sam walked into the dining room of his parents' house, grinning, Millie and Josh right behind him.

"Oh, how wonderful! I'll grab some more plates." Kathy cried, jumping out of her seat.

"Wait, mum, I wanted to tell you something first." Sam stopped his mum. He reached across and took Millie's hand, pulling her to his side as three stunned faces looked on. "Shall you tell them darling, or will I?" Sam asked Millie.

"You tell them."

"Mum, Dad, Josh...Millie and I are engaged!" Stunned silence followed his announcement. "For real this time," Sam added as an afterthought, Millie flashing her engagement ring.

A cheer erupted, Millie was engulfed by Kathy, as Sam was congratulated by his dad and Josh.

"It will be a quick engagement; we were hoping to marry on Valentine's Day," Millie added. Sam pulled Millie in for a kiss. He had told her, confessed to her that he had been so caught up the first night that they made love, that he had forgotten to use protection, and Millie had smiled at him, whispering that she couldn't wait to start a family with him, whatever the timing.

"That's only six weeks away!" Kathy's eyes grew large. "Is there something else you need to tell us?"

"No Kathy, you're not going to be a grandma just yet." Millie smiled. "We just don't want to wait for a second longer for our forever to start." Millie reached up to kiss Sam. She would never have imagined four weeks ago that she would have had both a fake fiancé and a real fiancé this Christmas, not in her wildest dreams.

It was funny how life worked out, the person she least expected had turned out to be her Mr Perfect, her happy ever after.

"I love you, husband to be." The truth of Millie's words shone out of her face like sunbeams, touching all of those who witnessed the declaration.

"I love you, wife to be." Sam's word carried a sincerity, an underlying rock solid truth that Millie never had cause to doubt, making this a Christmas to remember forever.

THE END

About The Author

An international bestselling and award-winning author of sweet contemporary romance, Kathleen's novels showcase thought-provoking plots and strong emotions that have been likened to a Hallmark movie. Featuring feisty heroines and strong heroes, where everyone gets a happily ever after. To discover more about Kathleen: Connect on social media

Read More of Kathleen's Books

The Flying Doctor's Christmas Wish
The Brooding Doctor's Christmas Wish
Christmas Wish Collection
The Surgeon's Baby
Fling With The Flying Doctor
The Marriage Deal
Caleb's Song
Cinnamon Kisses and Gingerbread Wishes